Real Friends

Real Friends

by Susan Sharpe

BRADBURY PRESS • NEW YORK

Maxwell Macmillan Canada • Toronto
Maxwell Macmillan International
New York • Oxford • Singapore • Sydney

Bradbury Press
Macmillan Publishing Company
866 Third Avenue
New York, NY 10022

Maxwell Macmillan Canada, Inc.
1200 Eglinton Avenue East
Suite 200
Don Mills, Ontario M3C 3N1

Macmillan Publishing Company is part of the
Maxwell Communication Group of Companies.
First edition
Printed in the United States of America

10 9 8 7 6 5 4 3 2 1
The text of this book is set in ITC New Baskerville.
Book design by Cathy Bobak

Library of Congress Cataloging-in-Publication Data

Sharpe, Susan.
Real friends / by Susan Sharpe. — 1st ed.
p. cm.
Summary: In a new school, fourteen-year-old Cassie finds her first
friend in the dynamic Helen, but Helen's attempt to claim her
exclusively threatens to bring bad consequences.
ISBN 0-02-782352-0
[1. Friendship—Fiction. 2. High schools—Fiction. 3. Schools—
Fiction.] I. Title.
PZ7.S5323Re 1994
[Fic]—dc20   94-14591

To Kati, Anne, Ellie,
and all the teens
who are friends in our house

Real Friends

1

XXX

Kids were drifting in waves across the street in front of the high school, toward the Roy Rogers and the Pizza Hut and the little shopping mall. Cassie stood on the step, gripping the strap of her heavy backpack. She knew lots of those kids' names already. There went Grace, who played on the basketball team and lived somewhere in the same direction as Cassie. And Sharon Newell, that loudmouth from English class, in her ridiculous little denim overall shorts and pink tights. Steve and Sharon were hurrying side by side, their heads bent down, laughing. Here came Sharon's pal Rebecca, in her green

1

Converse. She brushed past Cassie without seeing her, not looking as she headed into the street. A car honked.

"Hey, Sharon, wait uuuup!" Rebecca paid no attention to the car. "Hey, Sharon, you got any money?"

Sharon finally turned. "Did you say money, honey?"

Rebecca's answer was lost among the other voices and the traffic. A conversation in Spanish drifted past Cassie. She took another step down. Senseless bits and fragments of talk drifted around her with the people.

"She's strict but she's nice."

"Who, Mrs. Simms?"

"Hey, move it, shortie."

Cassie jumped. That one was to her. "Oh, shut up," she said, but the speaker had already passed out of earshot. She turned to the right at the bottom of the steps. She had been at this school for two months. Two months, and not a soul cared about her, or seemed to know who she was. Two months, with three years and seven months left to go. And to think that she had wanted this, had looked forward to this—to finally living in the United States and going to a real American school for high school.

Her father had a military career. They had lived in Panama, in Germany, in Egypt, in Germany again. Her parents often changed their minds about schools; sometimes there was a base school, sometimes they sent Cassie to a local public school, sometimes they found a private school. Always, Cassie was not understanding the language, or the customs, or the jokes, or else she was just moving again. But now her parents had promised: four years, one place, an American school.

"Cassie, hey, Cassie!"

Someone was calling her name, but Cassie didn't want to turn around, because she knew who it was. Susan Carpenter had started sitting next to her as soon as she realized that Cassie was also a good student. Susan got straight As by memorizing every single thing the teachers handed out, word for word. There was something about Susan. You could tell she did everything she was told, even brushed her teeth three times a day. Every afternoon Susan called Cassie "just to check" to make sure she was doing all her homework and getting all the answers right.

"Hey, Cassie." It was useless to pretend she didn't hear anymore, so Cassie turned. Susan's face was anxious.

"What's the matter?" Cassie asked reluctantly.

"I did terrible on the biology exam," Susan said with a quaver.

"But it's not your fault," said Cassie. "Everybody did bad. It was the wrong exam. He keeps them all in the filing cabinet and he just took the wrong one out. Don't you remember when Amal tried to tell him?"

"I know it's stupid," Susan admitted. "I know I shouldn't feel this way about a B minus."

Cassie didn't know what to say. She privately agreed with Susan that it was stupid to feel that way. "I only got a B plus," she said.

"But you don't mind. Oh, I wish I could be like you," Susan whined.

But my problem is different, Cassie thought. My problem is that I can't stand the idea that I *might* be like you in any way at all.

Fortunately Susan had to run for her bus, and now Cassie could walk home alone. The fall weather was mild in Virginia, and Cassie watched the trees as they changed colors. It had rained earlier and cleared the air, and now the sun lit up a row of bright yellow hickory trees. Behind her came three guys in leather jackets who lived in the apartments at the bottom of Wakefield Street. They were speaking Spanish; Cassie tried to pick out the words, but they spoke too fast, and their accent was different from the one in Panama.

She knew their names, too, because two of them were in her biology class. The good-looking one was Ricardo. He nodded as they went past her, but Cassie couldn't tell whether that was because he recognized her, or he was just being polite.

The guys turned in at the apartments and Cassie had started up the hill when a female voice called, "Hey, girl!"

Keeping her head down, Cassie glanced to right and left. There was no one else around; it must be a voice from inside the apartments. A lot of the windows were open.

"Hey! You with the book bag! Look up!"

Cassie looked up, and there was a face at a window.

"Yeah, it's me. I'm new. My name is Helen. You're coming from the high school, right?"

Cassie nodded.

"Wait a minute!"

It was a peremptory command, and Cassie wasn't sure that she would wait. She felt self-conscious, but there was no one around, really, just a man carrying groceries and a woman walking to her car. Cassie waited until a door opened, and out came Helen.

Helen was grinning. She had long stringy blond hair and beautiful blue eyes, and she was wearing jeans and a bright purple knit shirt and green Converse sneakers, just like Rebecca. She didn't wear any makeup and she didn't hesitate.

"Hi, hope you don't mind me stopping you, I saw you yesterday. We just got here. We're from Minnesota. Guess I'll be going to school tomorrow. So, you want to walk together?"

For a moment Cassie thought she meant to walk somewhere right now, and she couldn't think what to say, but Helen went on talking.

"What time do you come by? I guess I don't want to be late the first day. Hey, this is great, you can tell me the names of all the kids and what about them and everything."

Cassie took a step backward. "I don't really know that many kids," she said cautiously.

"Yeah, how come?"

Cassie almost felt dizzy for a second. It was a question she couldn't afford to ask herself. How come, indeed? Was it only because she was new? How come only Susan Carpenter ever talked to her? "I'm kind of new myself," she managed to say.

"Yeah? Really? Wow, what a coincidence. So, it's supposed to be a really great school, huh? Is it hard?"

How could Cassie possibly know what would be hard for this person? "Not that hard," she said.

"Well, that's good, anyway. So, what's your name?" Helen sat down on the little brick wall that edged the apartment grounds, but Cassie remained standing.

"Cassie."

"Like, for Cassandra?"

"Yes."

"Wow, another coincidence, huh? Helen, Cassandra. Two Greek ladies, both bad news."

Cassie heard herself giggle. She had never before met a kid who knew who Cassandra was. Her heart lifted suddenly.

"It's my birthday," said Cassie suddenly. She hadn't told a single person in school.

"Is that right? So, what, are you fourteen, or what?"

"Yes, fourteen."

"Hey, that's formidable. So many coincidences. I mean I was fourteen in August. Hey, you want to come in or anything?"

Cassie started to say yes, and then hesitated. She didn't want to go in and meet someone's family. And yet she liked Helen. She was supposed to invite someone home for her birthday dinner. What if she asked Helen? But wouldn't that be too personal, for someone you had just met? Helen would likely say no. "I have to go home and walk my little brother," Cassie said, hearing the disappointment in her own voice.

"What, he's a dog or something?"

Cassie laughed. "No, he's three. He goes to day

care. My mom says they don't go outdoors enough so he has to be taken for a walk in the afternoon. They get home around four. And then she goes shopping and does housework and stuff."

Helen shrugged. "Okay. See you tomorrow, okay? What time?"

"About a quarter to eight, I guess."

"Okay, look for me, I'll be here." Helen stood up and Cassie turned to walk up the hill. She wanted to look back and see if Helen was watching her, but she didn't want Helen to see her looking back, so she didn't.

Cassie got home before her mother. She put the breakfast bowls into the dishwasher, wondering whether Helen had to help with the housework. This was Cassie's best daydreaming time of day, pretending she was grown up and this was her own house. In one of her favorite dreams she was a heart surgeon. Now she looked down, and saw that the patient was her old friend from high school, Helen. "Trust me," Cassie said, holding the scalpel behind her back so as not to frighten her. "I'm so glad it's you," murmured Helen. Cassie nodded at the anesthetist, and unconsciousness closed Helen's blue

9

eyes. There was a fumbling scratchy sound of the key in the lock, and then the bright sound of Jamie's voice. The dream curled up inside Cassie like a woolly bear caterpillar.

"Hello, Cassie dear, happy birthday, how was school?" her mother asked. "Can you take one of these bags?"

"Hello, Cassie dear," said Jamie, in sincere imitation. "Happy birthday." He was carrying the bread, squishing it badly.

"It was okay. You want me to take him for a walk?"

"Yes, go out, it's turned into a lovely day. Watch out for the puddles."

Sometimes, Cassie thought, her mother spoke to her and Jamie as if they were the same age. She liked to get away with Jamie. He didn't think they were the same age; he gave her his hand, trustingly. He was interested in squirrels and tiny bits of trash, and he always went straight to the puddles. Cassie didn't stop him.

He had a regular game. He would stand six feet from a likely puddle, take aim, and yell, "One, two, three, puddles!" running pell-mell and splashing the thing into nonexistence. Cassie was glad. How many people were ever as happy as Jamie in a puddle? So what if someone had to wash his clothes.

"It's your birthday, Cassie," he reminded her, when the good puddles were all gone. "We're having *cake!*" His eyes shone with joy.

"Did Mommy buy a cake?"

"*And* candles. You get many, many candles!" He waved his arms as if the number were beyond all counting.

"That's good."

"Don't you like cake, Cassie?"

"Sure, I like cake."

When they returned to the house, their father was home. He had a little box, nicely wrapped, the way they do it in department stores. He gave Cassie a kiss on the cheek. "Happy birthday, Cassie."

"Thanks, Dad."

"Did you invite a friend over for dinner, the way your mother suggested?"

Cassie looked down at Jamie, who was driving a truck along the stripe in the kitchen tile. "I don't have any friends, Dad, remember?"

"Now, Cassie, I don't like to hear you talking like

11

that," said her mother. "I used to have so many wonderful friends in high school. Those are the golden years. That nice girl Susan Carpenter calls you several times a day, sometimes. Why didn't you ask her?"

"She just wants to talk about homework."

"Well, at your age, I think that's a very appropriate thing to talk about."

"Boys, too," said her father, winking at her. He took a bottle of white wine out of the refrigerator. "I bet they talk about boys, too."

Cassie had a hard time smiling. She felt that her parents were right; other people had friends in high school, but Cassie could not figure out how to do it, and her parents could not understand her problem. They had no idea what it felt like to be a nobody at a new school and not to have any real friends, no one who cared about you.

After dinner they gave her presents. There were several books and a new tennis racket, and the little box from her father turned out to be earrings. They were a surprise; her father had never given her real silver jewelry, and they dangled in twin spirals that looked like DNA. Cassie tried them on and laughed. Her mother gave her a new blouse, an expensive one, covered with blue flowers, with a sweet round collar edged with lace. Cassie hated it immediately, but she went upstairs and dutifully tried it on. She looked like a nobody. Nobody at school wore sweet round collars.

She thanked her parents and hugged them, because they did care about her, even if their way of caring didn't seem to do her any good. She went to her room and did her homework. Susan Carpenter called and they went over the answers to the algebra problems, and then Cassie went to bed.

In the dark, even more than in the empty house, she could always imagine friends. She even heard their conversations; she saw places they would go. She and this girl, maybe it was Helen, were going into the District to visit the art museums. They were dropping into a little Vietnamese restaurant. They didn't know what to order, when two older guys came in, about eighteen years old. They were from Great Britain. They said, hey, we'll join you. Then they were all laughing about the menu.

Sometimes, when she was almost asleep, Cassie thought about Ricardo. This time she dreamed that the school was burning down. Orange flames rose angrily into the sky, and little bodies of firemen who looked like her father appeared at smoky windows, or caught in dangerous stairwells. Sirens wailed, teachers screamed, and Helen's face appeared serenely at a window, then disappeared in smoke. Ricardo picked Cassie up, holding her close to him, carrying her out of the building, cherishing her, caring about her.

2

*M*r. *Raffensberger plunged his veined hand deep* into the clear glass jar of sheep's eyes, scowling at the class. His arthritic fingers paddled in the thick liquid that held the eyes like big marbles, their pale blue pupils turning slowly around and around as he failed to grasp one.

Kalisha shrieked, while two of Ricardo's friends, who were sitting on the backs of their chairs, began bleating through cupped hands. They always kept their leather jackets on in school, Cassie noticed. Not because it was cold—it was hot and stuffy—but just to signal how temporarily they felt themselves

15

to be here, as if they were in a store and might leave at any moment. Cassie did not feel like them at all. She felt as if she would be sitting here for the rest of her life, in her stupid new shirt that she had worn to please her mother.

What could have happened to the girl at the apartments? Cassie had waited for ten minutes, until she was sure she was going to be late. Maybe Helen had lied about going to school, maybe she was just visiting. Maybe she was really going to a parochial school. Maybe she had met someone in the apartments she would rather walk with, and they had left earlier without waiting for Cassie.

Cassie hated this class more than ever. Mr. Raffensberger was too old to be trying to teach. He couldn't handle the class and he couldn't remember what he was doing from one day to the next, or sometimes even in the middle of class. He finally got hold of an eyeball and held it up. It dripped a bit of stringy liquid, which made half the girls squeal again. "All right now, this is the eye," he said in his thin, high, uncertain voice. "You have to learn the parts of the eye." It didn't matter what the words were, Mr. Raffensberger always sounded as if no one would ever have to do anything.

"The parts of the eye," Mr. Raffensberger continued. "Page . . ." But he had forgotten the page.

"Two hundred and twelve," said Cassie, louder than she had intended.

A dozen heads whirled around and looked at her.

"Huh," said the boy next to Ricardo. "Two hundred and twelve, stupid." He knocked his other neighbor's baseball cap off. "How come you didn't know that? She knows that. You know her? She gets As. Not like you, stupid." All three boys began to hoot in shrill voices, while Mr. Raffensberger made ineffectual shushing noises.

Cassie bent her head over the page and looked at the diagram of the eye. The retina was a thin red line in an oval. At the front of the eye was a lens and then a pupil surrounded by iris, covered by a cornea. The diagram showed how an image entered the eye and landed upside down on the retina. There was a picture of a little chair outside the eye, and then a tiny upside-down chair inside the eye, with crossing dotted lines to show what happened.

That was interesting, but it was not quite right. You could never see just a chair. When you opened your eyes, it was always a jumble of things together, bits of chairs, an ear with a tiny gold ring, a rattail, a Reebok, Susan Carpenter's curly hair blocking the brightly colored chart of the vertebrates that Mr. Raffensberger had actually neglected to take down for the vertebrate exam. Did your eye turn everything over equally, all the scraps and fragments? It was a funny idea, the whole room spilling headlong as if in an earthquake. Cassie smiled to herself. Think how surprised everyone would be if they knew she longed for earthquakes and fires, just to get her out of this.

After biology, there was Latin. In some ways Latin was the best class. It was small, most of the students were older than Cassie, and by some grace of nature Susan Carpenter was taking French. It was quiet and orderly, with a teacher who seemed mild and civilized, who treated the students politely. And the work had enchanted Cassie from the start. *Agricola,* farmer. Like a quiet little joke. Of course, you did have to memorize endings, and then you had to understand grammar. That was the hardest part. But it was like a puzzle. Sometimes two different cases had the same ending, and you had to figure out which meaning would work. Cassie liked it, although she was not especially interested in Caesar.

She sat near the back, listening to Steve do his translation. "Caesar over the field marched with twenty legions having spoken to the commanders." Mrs. Simms said that was very good, but could anyone change the word order to help it flow more smoothly in English?

Cassie smiled at her neighbor, a thin Korean girl named Connie. "Caesar marched," Cassie mouthed at her.

"What?" Connie looked surprised.

"Nothing." Cassie shrugged.

Peter Hofnagle did the sentence over. "Having spoken to his commanders, Caesar marched over the field with twenty legions." That was even better than Cassie's idea, and she wrote the new sentence in her notebook, feeling Connie's eyes on her.

"You like Latin, don't you?" Connie asked.

"Yeah, it's okay."

"Weird." Connie stared back at her book.

When the bell rang, Connie left her seat abruptly to join her friends in the hallway. Cassie didn't care about them, either. She went to her locker, alone as usual. And yet she found herself looking, up and down the hall, watching the people as she put away the morning's books.

Instead of Helen she saw Rebecca Goldman, who had a locker next to hers but had too many friends of her own to bother talking to Cassie. And yet today she spoke. Maybe it had to do with the way Cassie was looking around. "You get new earrings?" Rebecca asked.

"It was my birthday yesterday," Cassie answered, averting her face.

"They're cool," Rebecca said. She wore huge round earrings herself, and dark lipstick. "Your mom give them to you?"

"No, my dad."

"Wow, my dad would never give me anything that cool. Hey, Sharon, come and look at Cassie's new earrings. Her dad gave them to her."

Cassie was uneasy. Were the earrings really cool,

or was Rebecca making fun of her? She pulled out her English book.

Sharon was paying no attention, anyway. She slammed her locker, opened it, and slammed it again louder. "This goddamn thing doesn't close right."

But Rebecca was persistent. "Your mom give you anything?"

"Yeah, she gave me this shirt."

Sharon looked up then, and laughed. "And you hate it, right?" she said.

This was so true that it took Cassie by surprise. She stared at Sharon a moment, but no words came out of her mouth.

"All right, so don't hate it. Go ahead and feel happy in your Laura Ashley miss snotty good-grades shirt." Sharon slammed her locker one last time and sped down the hallway to her next class.

"Never mind her," said Rebecca. "She's in trouble in a couple of her classes, and her parents are hassling her."

"Oh." The warning bell rang, and Rebecca began to run. But Cassie slipped into the bathroom, which was empty now. She looked at herself in the one dirty mirror, but she couldn't seem to see herself. There was her face, with the brown eyes like the eyes of a little girl, no makeup, no glasses, just there in her face like stupid dots. There was her brown hair with the gold highlights, and yet it didn't look right, did it? There was the flash of silver dangling against her cheek. There was the round blue collar, and the lace. Other girls looked like something: they were skinny or fat, they were cute or beautiful or even ugly, but each girl had something, some look. She tried to remember what Helen looked like, but even though she said "blue eyes" to herself, she couldn't recall the face. She felt like a mannequin, dressed up in her parents' presents. She couldn't bear to see it anymore, so she left for English class.

She was late, which might have meant that the whole class would watch her taking her seat, but as soon as she reached the door she saw she was lucky. Class hadn't really started yet, because someone was standing next to Mr. McCutcheon at the front of the room. Cassie passed in quickly behind her and sat down.

"That's A block. This is B block, okay? Isn't that

what you call it here? Isn't this B block? Isn't this room one twenty-three?"

Who else had a voice like that, loud enough to stop a pedestrian from the third floor? It was Helen, and in another minute she was going to notice Cassie.

"All right, all right, then let me get your name down on my roll." Mr. McCutcheon was trying to find a pen in the disorder on top of his desk. "One *l* or two?"

"My first name is Helen. One *l*." Helen looked up at the class and rolled her eyes, but when she saw Cassie, she broke into a grin and waved enthusiastically.

"I *know* how to spell Helen. Spell your last name for me." It was one of Mr. McCutcheon's short-tempered days.

"One *l*. Like it says there. Holsinger. *H-o-l-s—*"

Mr. McCutcheon waved at her impatiently, but Helen didn't seem to mind him a bit. She pointed happily at the empty seat next to Cassie, who nodded vigorously.

"All right, I believe there's an empty seat back there, you can take that."

Helen bustled back and sat down, speaking only somewhat more quietly to Cassie. "Sorry about this morning. My mother had to bring me. Can you imagine that, high school, and a parent has to bring you. Jeez, if they knew my mother, I should bring *her*."

Cassie wondered what was the matter with Helen's mother, but she didn't have time to ask, because Helen kept talking. "Quite a coincidence, wouldn't you say? Both of us in the same English class. Jeez, I thought I'd never see you today. I mean, this school is *huge*."

"It must be a lot bigger than your school in Minnesota."

Mr. McCutcheon cleared his throat. He was standing with his book open now. "Perhaps you could welcome our new friend at some more appropriate time," he chided Cassie, but she didn't care. She opened her book, smiling.

"You have a book yet?" she asked Helen.

"No, let's share, hey, you doing poetry? That's cool. Who's this, Emily Dickinson? Jeez, that's easy. We did that in eighth grade."

Mr. McCutcheon harrumphed again. "Perhaps

you are not aware, Ms. Holsinger, that we do not carry on conversations in the middle of class. You are now in the middle of class. Will you read to us, please. From page seventy-three. You will stand to read, please."

You could tell that he was hoping to embarrass Helen, but to Cassie's delight he was in for a surprise. Helen stood and read forcefully, raising her eyes from the page as if she almost knew the poem by heart.

I'm Nobody! Who are you?
Are you—Nobody—Too?
Then there's a pair of us?
Don't tell! they'd advertise—you know!

. . . . .

How dreary—to be—Somebody!
How public—like a Frog—
To tell one's name—the livelong June—
To an admiring Bog!

Cassie watched Helen while she read. Her blond hair was long and unstyled, just like Cassie's. Her blue eyes were without makeup, but they did not look like dots in her face; they looked refreshing and bold and right. She was wearing the same clothes as yesterday; she didn't need to dress up for this place, even if she was new.

"That's very nice," said Mr. McCutcheon when she had finished, unable to disguise the admiration in his voice. "I see you have studied poetry previously."

"Emily Dickinson is one of my favorites," said Helen. Cassie could hear several sniggers from around the room, but Helen didn't appear to care. "Also," she said loudly, "my father used to write poetry."

"My, my, isn't that wonderful." Mr. McCutcheon was so impressed that he had forgotten his usual boring lecture about what the poem means, the part of class that often made Cassie ache with impatience. Instead he asked a boy named Kevin to read the next one.

Kevin read very badly, so that you could tell he didn't understand any of it. Helen rolled her eyes at Cassie. "I thought this was supposed to be a great school," she whispered.

"It is. Supposed to be." Cassie giggled, and

caught Mr. McCutcheon frowning at her again. When he began to write on the board, she leaned over toward Helen. "Want to go somewhere after school?"

Helen's eyes brightened. "Definitely."

"We could go over to Roy's. You know, over on the highway?"

"Formidable."

Mr. McCutcheon was explaining that Emily Dickinson lived alone in an upstairs bedroom and sent messages down in a basket. It might have been interesting yesterday, but now Cassie couldn't wait until the end of school.

3

Cassie waited for Helen, as planned, at her locker after school. Rebecca came and grabbed a jacket and ran off without speaking this time, but Cassie did not mind. She was waiting for someone, someone smarter and more interesting than Rebecca, anyway. The hall was packed with bodies at first, but gradually open spaces appeared. Cassie changed her mind about bringing her English book home, and then waited again, shifting her weight from foot to foot. Mr. McCutcheon passed and smiled at her. Mr. Raffensberger walked by, nodded, and said,

"Hello, Susan." Cassie stuck out her tongue at his back.

At last she saw Helen, her purple shirt weaving down the yellow hallway under the dim lights.

"Hey, glad I found you. This place is huge. They gave me a locker way up on the third floor, with the seniors. How many kids go to this school, anyway? Seems like there's thousands of them. Hey, I hear you get good grades."

Cassie was astonished. "How did you hear that?"

"I asked this girl, Susan Carpenter. I saw her with you this morning. She said you get practically the best grades in the whole school. That's just like me, actually I was valedictorian at the school where I was. Or I would have been, by the time I graduated. So, you ready for Roy's? Looks like this place has cleared out already."

Together, Helen and Cassie went down the school steps and across the street. There were two fast-food places, one block down along the highway, but Roy's was closer. Cassie had never been to it, but she'd heard kids talking, and she knew they went there.

"You hungry?" she asked Helen.

"Sure, always. Didn't get much lunch. We haven't really had time to get groceries yet. I just grabbed a hot dog from home for lunch."

"You can buy lunch, you know."

"Yeah, well, I have to wait for my mom to get meal tickets."

"Meal tickets? You don't get tickets here, you just get in line and buy whatever you want. It's not that great, maybe, but they have a salad bar, it's not too bad."

Helen mumbled something.

"What?"

"I said, *we* have to get meal tickets, okay? You get a discount that way."

Cassie felt herself go pink with shame. Of course, she knew that some kids used tickets, she had seen them. She just had never really thought about what for.

"I'm sorry," she said. "But what about Roy's? That costs a lot more than school lunch."

"I'll just have a soda or something."

"But you said you were hungry."

"Well, I'm not a starving Somali or anything, okay?"

Cassie got pink again. "Let me get you something."

Helen laughed. "Okay. As soon as my mother gets a job, I'll pay you back."

The Roy Rogers smelled of french fries and onions. Cassie suddenly felt amazingly hungry. "I'm starved, actually," she said. "How about we each get a hamburger?"

"Sure."

Cassie looked around surreptitiously while a guy filled their order. Nearly everyone at the tables was from the high school. Rebecca and Sharon were at a table with Grace and two other kids that Cassie didn't know. They were making a lot of noise, playing a game with pennies and paper cups. Pennies kept falling on the floor.

"I thought I was the only one who hates Isaac," Sharon was saying. Cassie didn't catch the reply, if there was one. Their hamburgers plopped onto the tray in front of them, and Helen scooped it up.

"Where to?" She waited for directions from Cassie.

Cassie didn't move, she just shrugged. There were some empty tables in the back, but she didn't like having to walk past everybody.

"Next!" said the guy behind the counter, and Helen gave her a little shove with the plastic tray. So Cassie led the way. Rebecca looked up and saw her, ran her eye up and down Helen, and turned back to the penny game. Grace said briefly, "Hi, Cassie." That was all. Then they were seated at a table against the back wall, under a picture of the Washington Monument.

Helen dived into her hamburger without another word. She must have been really hungry, Cassie thought, as she ate hers more slowly.

"Okay, so when did you get here?" Helen finally asked, when most of her burger had disappeared.

"In the fall. I started in September. Most of these kids went to middle school together. They're kind of cliquey, you know what I mean?"

"I noticed that. You're the only one who's at all open, like to anyone new. Where'd you get the cool earrings?" Helen asked, fixing her gaze on Cassie's left ear.

"My dad."

"Formidable. What's he like?"

"He's okay. He works at the Pentagon. He's the reason we always moved around so much. He's pretty straight. No poetry." Cassie looked at Helen, hoping to hear more about her family, but Helen brushed the subject away.

"Where'd you get the shirt? That him, too?"

"No, that's my mom."

"Don't tell me, she's straight, too. *Very* straight. She keeps little color-coordinated shell-shaped soaps in the bathroom, and she's an officer in the PTA."

Cassie burst out laughing. "Not *that* straight. She works most of the time, she's a career counselor for people who are out of work. She's just straight when she buys things for me, I don't know. I probably should like this shirt, but I just don't."

"Of *course* you don't. It's not you at all. I mean, it's obvious your mother doesn't understand you, at all. I've only known you for a day, and I would *never* buy you that shirt. You want to know what I think you should wear? First of all, no flowers, and dark colors. No lace. No round collars. More like a man-tailored shirt, maybe the outdoor look. Hey, you want to go shopping? We could find out what looks good on you."

Cassie had never been shopping with a friend. Most of her clothes were purchased by her mother, sometimes by mail order, or else at the PX on the base. Looking around the high school, she knew that most of what she owned was wrong, but it was hard to learn to shop in American stores all at once. And she was always with her mother, who was always in a hurry. "That's nice," she would say. "Green or blue? Hurry up, Cassie, I've got to get some new shirts for Jamie, too."

"Yes, let's go," Cassie said. The other kids were gone already, and Cassie and Helen slipped out of Roy's and across the highway, dodging in front of a Metrobus. There was a tiny little mall that must have been built there twenty years ago, but it had several clothing stores. There were sale signs in some of the windows.

The first window had mannequins dressed in

wool suits. Cassie paused to look at them, but Helen shoved her away. "Not that stuff, stupid."

"I know, I know, I'm just looking." Still, Cassie felt stupid. This was not at all like looking at an L.L. Bean catalog.

The next window, past the jeweler's, had no mannequins, only piles of sweaters and shirts in the window, in dark fall colors. The shirts had pointed collars, Cassie noticed.

"Looks like the place," said Helen.

"Right," Cassie answered, feeling foolishly excited. "Let's go in."

There were piles of turtlenecks on tables, at one-third off. There were racks of shiny shirts with floral and geometric patterns. There were patterned cotton pants, made wide at the hips, and there was a whole wall of socks in wonderful colors. Helen led the way around.

"This isn't much better than the Cities," Helen said. "We have all these styles. I thought in the east there'd be a lot more stuff. This is all the old stuff. Hey, that's a nice pattern, don't you love it?"

Helen had pulled out a pair of the cotton pants with a vivid swirling pattern in purple and dark blue. Cassie looked at it dubiously. Did she love it? Maybe, in a way. "I usually wear jeans," she said.

"You ought to get some that, like, fit a little better than that," said Helen. Cassie was hurt for a moment. She looked at Helen's jeans, a little too tight to be comfortable.

"Ooh, look at these." Helen was handling a rack of silk scarves, 10 percent off. They had hot colors, orange and red and pink. She held one up to her neck. "How do I look?"

A salesgirl, not much older than they were, looked condescendingly at Helen. "Can I help you with something today?"

"We're just looking," answered Helen professionally. The salesgirl looked bored and left them alone.

"I saw some girls wearing these," said Cassie, standing in front of a rack of short pleated plaid skirts. Her mother never gave her enough time to just look at things and think about them. She found the skirts cute, peppy. She thought maybe she had nice legs, and would look good in a short skirt. Not that she would want anyone to think she was dressing up for them. She turned away.

"Only weenies wear plaids," Helen announced, and the two of them began to giggle.

"Sometimes my father wears plaid pants," Cassie remembered.

"Oh, contemptible. I hate men who do that. Don't you hate it?"

"For sure." Cassie's gaze wandered over the hats, little round black things. Then she stopped at a white shirt. There was only one. It had gathering at the shoulders to make puffy sleeves, wide, buttoned cuffs, a long, pointed collar, and many tiny tucks running down the front. It looked like the shirt a Shakespearean actor would wear, or maybe George Washington. "Look, Helen," she said.

"*Ooooh*, it's formidable. Isn't it formidable, Cass? And it's really *you*. That's what you look good in. What size is it? Try it on."

Cassie looked carefully at the label, the way her mother would. SQUARE ONE, BEAUTIFUL CLOTHES. 60% POLYESTER, 40% COTTON. MACHINE WASH.

"Look at the tag on the sleeve," Helen suggested. This one said, SIZE 6 $39.95. It had been marked down from $49.95.

Cassie lifted it down from the rack and held it up

against herself in the mirror. She loved it, the way it was cut like a man's shirt, the way the fabric flowed around, the pointed collar. She grinned, looking at Helen behind her. "Okay, where's a dressing room?"

The salesgirl appeared from nowhere with a key in her hand, and let them into a very small cubicle with a mirror.

"Well, one difference between here and the Cities, they sure don't trust you here," Helen volunteered. "Did you notice all the shoplifting signs? I feel like they're going to clap me in handcuffs if I look at them cross-eyed. Did you notice how the girl was watching us?"

Cassie was too busy buttoning the shirt to answer. The buttons were pearl and felt nice.

"For sure," said Helen, when she was finished.

Cassie agreed with her. She felt transformed. She looked in the mirror, and she was somebody. Not nobody, not even part of a pair of nobodies. She had a nice figure, and soft brown hair that only needed to be trimmed. Her eyes were soft brown, too, and her skin looked just right with the ivory shade of the shirt. She realized, now, that light blue made her look sick.

"So, you going to get it?" Helen asked.

"I can't. I don't have forty dollars. I already spent three bucks at Roy's." She did have a twenty, though, folded into her book bag, that her parents wanted her to keep for emergencies. And she had a ten of her own money, that she didn't usually carry around but that she had put into her wallet this morning, who knows why, just because she was hoping to meet up with Helen.

"So how much do you have? Maybe a credit card or something? Besides, wasn't that shirt on the twenty-five-percent-off table?"

"No, and anyway it's already been marked down." Cassie began taking it off, reluctantly. The thought of shoplifting even crossed her mind momentarily. Her mother would never buy her that shirt.

"Why don't you ask, anyway?"

"I don't need to ask, the price is marked, right here. See?" Cassie held the tag out.

But Helen took the shirt from her, undaunted. "I'll ask," she said. "Just put your old blue meanie back on, and I'll go ask."

Cassie came out in time to hear the salesgirl say

she'd check. She disappeared through a door and was gone for minutes, leaving them staring at the hot scarves and the patterned pants. Maybe another day, Cassie thought, she would try some of the pants on. She would need something to wear with the shirt. Except she couldn't afford the shirt. She felt uncomfortable, thinking how she would have to tell the salesgirl it was too much.

The girl returned, looking more polite. "It's the last one," she said. "So the manager just marked it down. It's $29.95. You want me to ring it up?"

What would the tax come to? How much, exactly, was in her wallet? She had used a five at Roy's, so there was some change from that. "Okay," said Cassie. "Ring it up." She smiled again at Helen, and on the way out she had to keep herself from skipping.

"So," said Helen, when they were back in the mall. "You want to come to my place? You can, like, meet my mother."

"And your dad, the poet?" This *was* a day of wonders.

"Well, not actually. He left quite a while ago.

My mom told me about the poetry. Which way is it, anyway?"

Cassie steered them back across the highway and up the hill in the direction of home. "I'm sorry about your dad. Does he visit you and everything?"

"No, actually, I'm not sure he knows I was born. I mean, he left a *long* time ago."

"So at least it's not like you actually miss him."

Helen didn't say anything, so Cassie went on talking. "My father is like, I don't know, I always get this idea he wishes I was someone else."

"How come?"

Cassie had never said that about her father before, and it was strange to hear the words. Did she really think that? She tried again.

"I mean he loves me and everything, but he thinks I should be real popular. My mom, too. They can't figure out why guys aren't asking me to the movies every weekend."

"That's ridiculous," said Helen stoutly.

Cassie smiled. "It is, isn't it?"

"Guys think girls are just falling all over to go out with them," said Helen. "I mean, I had this

41

boyfriend in Minnesota, and he was like, I *know* how much you're gonna miss me. Ha, ha. I don't miss him. He's probably making out with some new girl right this minute."

"Oh, but maybe not! Would he really do that? So soon?" Cassie asked.

Helen kicked at some dry leaves. "I guess you don't know guys the way I do," she said.

Cassie silently assented to this, and felt glad that her new friend had some experience. She wanted to ask several questions about what it was like having a boyfriend, but she didn't want to pry too soon. They approached the apartments. "Did you have a house in Minnesota?" Cassie asked.

"Lord no. We lived with relatives. This is supposed to be our big break. So, you want to come by?"

"Well, what time is it?" Helen had a watch.

"About a quarter to five."

"Really? No, is it really? Oh wow. My mom might be home already."

"So, your mother will be home. What's the big deal?"

"Well, yeah, but, it's just, she doesn't know where I am."

"Well, neither does mine. You shouldn't let your mother get in your way like that."

There wasn't much to be done about it now, and anyway, Cassie figured, probably Helen was right. Her mother had never laid down any rules about coming home, not this year. She was in high school, after all. It was time to do as she pleased. And her mother would be so glad to hear she had a friend.

"I think I better go home, though," Cassie answered. "I'll definitely come another time. Maybe we can get together this weekend."

"Definitely." Helen gave Cassie a warm hug, and Cassie strolled happily on up the street, swinging her store bag. Wait till she told her mother what a great bargain it was, too.

The front door was open, and Jamie was playing with his plastic figures on the rug. "Hi, Jamie!"

He looked at her with wrinkled brow, in perfect imitation of their mother when she was cross. "Where were you, Cassie?" he asked reproachfully.

She kneeled down beside him, dropping her bag. "Is that what Mom said?"

"You didn't take me for a walk."

She picked up a ghastly figure of an alien with

green teeth. "I bought a new shirt instead," she said, walking the alien along the carpet.

"Is that you, Cassie?" Her mother came tapping into the room, still in her work shoes. "It's past five o'clock, sweetie. I wondered where you were."

That didn't sound too bad. "I went shopping, after school."

"Oh, did you? It's a good thing I didn't get home earlier, I would have been worried. Susan called. Come and help me put this laundry away." She took her shoes off, one at a time, placing them on the stairs to go up.

Cassie followed her to the little laundry room off the kitchen, and began folding her father's T-shirts into a neat pile. "There's a new girl in school," she began. "She's, like, formidable."

"Leave these things out, that's going upstairs to Jamie's room," said her mother. "Here's your stuff, you can take it up when you go." She looked at Cassie keenly. "What sort of a girl?"

What a weird question. "A nice girl, Mom."

"Where's she from?"

"Minnesota."

"And where'd you go shopping?"

"In that little mall that's right across King Street, you know, on the other side of school."

"Oh, that little place. Well, sweetie, that's not a very good place to shop. Why don't you let me know the next time you need something? What is it you need, anyway?"

"A shirt." Cassie backed into the kitchen.

"But I just got you a shirt." Her mother's head was almost in the dryer, but Cassie heard an edge of annoyance creep into her voice.

"I know, and thanks. It's nice. But I just found one that I loved. I used the twenty dollars that you gave me for emergencies. It was a really good price, almost fifty percent off. I'll give you some of my baby-sitting money to pay for it. Okay?"

Her mother came out of the laundry room, a pile of shirts in one hand, looking at Cassie. "You mean this new girl led you over there and persuaded you to buy something?"

"Wait till you see it, Mom. It's, like, formidable." Cassie knew she was using Helen's word, but why not?

"Well, hey, Ms. Formidable, go try it on and show us then." Her mother turned her back and began taking out pots to cook dinner. "Don't forget to take your clothes up with you."

Cassie ran upstairs, balancing the store bag on top of her pile of underwear and socks. She put the shirt on gently, enjoying the smell of new fabric. When she stood in front of the mirror, she still loved it. Jamie came in and peeked in the mirror behind her.

"Like it, James?" She fluttered her arms so the wide sleeves flowed through the air.

"It's funny," he said seriously.

Cassie went downstairs and into the kitchen, where her mother burst out laughing. "Some new friend!" she said. Then she laughed again. "Well, I guess people have to make their mistakes."

Without answering, Cassie spun on her heel and went back upstairs. She looked in the mirror. Her mother was wrong. Absolutely wrong. The shirt was wonderful. Her mother probably didn't want her to look good, anyway. That was probably the real reason behind the blue shirt with the round collar— her mother actually wanted her to look like a jerk.

Cassie realized she didn't have Helen's telephone number. If she had it, she would have called, right then and there. Tomorrow she was going to wear her own shirt to school and she was going to find out everything about Helen, why her father left and why they came to Washington and what her mother was like. They could really trade some notes on mothers.

She put on an old L.L. Bean stripy turtleneck for dinner. There was no point taking chances getting food on the new shirt.

4

Helen was not in English the next morning. The class schedule got rotated on different days, just to confuse everybody; maybe Helen had gotten confused. Cassie sat there next to the empty desk, feeling naked in her new shirt, listening to Sharon trying to pretend she had done her homework. "I *read* it, Mr. McCutcheon. It's just, I don't know why, poetry has always been, like, real hard for me. So I didn't understand too much. But I read it. I read it twice."

Mr. McCutcheon asked Grace if she perhaps had a better understanding than her friend. He was sneering at them both. Cassie was annoyed with him. He should be trying to teach them, not proving how much smarter he was.

Miguel had his hand up, waving it like a little kid. He couldn't contain himself any longer. "I know, Mr. McCutcheon. It's about making choices, isn't it? The two roads, like two choices. And him, he's a poet, so he takes the road less traveled by. Is that right?"

"Very good, Miguel. Now I want everyone to turn to your notes about metaphor. Pamela, what is a metaphor?"

The door opened and Helen came in. Making no apology, she walked directly to her seat and noisily opened her book bag.

"I beg your pardon, Miss, uh—" He looked at the papers on his desk, but couldn't find the right one. Then he remembered. "Miss Holsinger. This is not the beginning of class."

"I know. I was seeing a counselor. Do you think you could call me Helen?"

"All right then, Helen, I want to hear your example of a metaphor from last night's reading."

"Well, there were quite a few of them. I suppose

the most obvious example is from the Frost poem "The Road Not Taken." He implies that the roads have some greater meaning. It could be life choices. You know, like if you follow the crowd, or you do something different."

Mr. McCutcheon looked quite surprised by all that, and so did half the class. "Excellent. Now, class, you notice she said there were quite a few metaphors. Perhaps someone could find one of the less obvious ones."

Helen turned to Cassie. "Nice shirt."

"My mother hates it," Cassie whispered. "What were you seeing a counselor for?"

"Too bad for your mother. She probably wears Villager skirts to work, right? I had to see a counselor. About the lunch tickets. And also, I changed my schedule."

"You did? I didn't know they would let you do that."

Helen passed over her blue schedule card triumphantly.

"Hey, now you're in my math class. And keyboarding. Formidable." Cassie laughed happily, and then she had to find the next metaphor.

"Can I come over after school?" Cassie asked, when she had slipped from Mr. McCutcheon's attention. "I have to tell you about my mother."

"Sure. And meet mine." Helen rolled her eyes once more, and Cassie stifled another laugh.

Cassie enjoyed the whole day. A couple of times she caught herself humming under her breath. Here she was, Cassandra Winn, having a good time. In school. When Susan Carpenter slid onto the bench beside them at lunchtime, they kept right on giggling about Mr. McCutcheon and laughing about Sharon's overalls. They laughed so hard in the halls that people looked at them, and Cassie was glad.

She got to biology a minute early, but she couldn't get into the room because one of the leather jacket boys was lounging in the doorway, his arm out to the opposite doorpost. Cassie paused in the hall, pretending to shuffle her books. She watched as one of the Middle Eastern students, Amal, walked up to the door, with two friends close behind.

"Outta the way, greaseball," Amal said. He sounded angry; there was some quarrel between them already.

"Who you callin' greasy, towel-head?" Manny smiled as he said this, without moving. Cassie remembered that Amal had worn a turban during the first weeks of school, although he no longer did.

"Latino trash," Amal announced loudly, turning to his friends, and immediately there seemed to be a gathering of kids in the hall. They lined up with their bodies, as if voting for Amal or voting for Manny, or just waiting, hoping for it to pass, like Cassie. She saw Mr. Raffensberger inside the room. He seemed to be gesturing with his hands, powerlessly, while no words came out of his mouth. Susan was already in there, sitting at her desk, watching the commotion with surprise.

"Hey, Manny," another leather jacket called from the hallway. "Can't hardly get through the door, too many dirty camel drivers."

Manny laughed, removed his arm, and squared his shoulder in the doorway.

"You just get outta the way," said Amal. He moved his body forward, too close to Manny, who kept smiling. Manny was about an inch taller than Amal.

"Hey, Mohammed, you wanna study with me?"

Amal raised his fist. In another second he was going to fight, and then what was going to happen? Cassie wished she had the courage to do something, but what?

"Hey, look everybody!" called a cheerful voice behind her. "The brain's got a new shirt."

Cassie whirled around to see Ricardo smiling at her.

"Hey, Manny, check out the babe." His words were rude, but his eyes were saying something else. "Hey, Manny, come on out, man, I gotta grab a smoke before class. You wanna smoke, babe?" He was not really speaking to Cassie, and in that instant she realized that he was using her to divert everyone's attention so that the fight or whatever would not take place.

"You asking *her*? She won't smoke with you. She's never even had a cigarette. Look at her." That was Manny, who had already left the doorway, and the groups were broken up. Amal passed muttering into the classroom.

"I'm asking her, not you," said Ricardo, looking

at Cassie. He winked, which might mean that he knew that she knew what was going on. But what should she say?

"Thanks," she managed. "I guess I better get to class, okay?"

"Oh yeah, can't be late," Ricardo agreed. And then as suddenly as he had paid attention to her, he stopped, and went into the room. Cassie felt her heart beating from a confusion of feelings. She would have to tell Helen about it; Helen was so certain of things, she would know what to think.

But after biology came Latin, and as she was headed in that direction she saw Ricardo again, at a water fountain. None of his friends was around him. With his head bent over to drink he didn't see her, but that in a way gave her more courage.

"That was a good thing you did."

He stood up suddenly, a drop of water falling from his lip to the floor. He stared at her, as if she were a creature from outer space who had no right to address him. Cassie cowered inside, but she remained standing there. Then he said, casually, "Don't mess with Manny. He gets kind of rough."

That made Cassie smile. "What would I mess with Manny for?"

Again, Ricardo stared at her. "You got anything against Spanish kids?"

"No, of course not." Now a flicker of anger shot through her. "I used to live in Panama. I went to school there."

She saw the light of surprise in his brown eyes. "How come?"

"My father's in the military. We lived a lot of places."

"Oh yeah." Was there disdain in his voice now? Maybe he didn't like military people. "But anyway," he said quickly, "it's really a good-looking shirt." Then he whirled away from her, the wrong direction for Latin class.

Cassie's heart flipped, and then she laughed at herself. If she ever did go out with a guy, it wouldn't be one of these kids, or at least she didn't think so. But why not? She knew a lot more about the world than any of the other kids at this contemptible school, didn't she? You never know. One friend had come to her.

Helen was waiting at Cassie's locker when school got out. "So, you want to go shopping again?"

"Are you kidding? I have to get more baby-sitting jobs first. I thought we were going over to your place."

"There's not much to see there."

"But I want to. I want to see where you live, and see your mother, and then the next day you can come and see mine. I have to know what you think about her. She didn't like my shirt. And we can take Jamie for a walk together."

"We could do that today. It's a pretty nice day."

"No, it isn't, it's cold. Your place first."

All the way home, Cassie tried to find an opening to talk about her mother and her encounters with Ricardo, but she found it difficult to start. Helen was chattering on about teachers and kids, doing imitations of the keyboarding teacher, whom she had met for the first time that day. "So very positive," Helen described her, in a voice that imitated the sugary tones that dripped over the word processors and old typewriters. "You know what she said to me when she called me up to her desk?" Helen added in her own voice. "I didn't proofread my exercise and it was full of mistakes, but she goes, 'Oh, Helen!'—changing to the drip-sweet voice— 'Oh, Helen, you have so much confidence!' Cassie couldn't help laughing; it caught Ms. Harkness perfectly. Nothing was ever just plain bad or sloppy or rude, everything had to have a positive face on it. She had smiley-face stickers for their exercises, and on her desk a sign that said, "Today is the first day of the rest of your life." Cassie secretly found the sign terrifying, but she supposed it seemed cheerful to adults, who have everything worked out.

"There was almost a fight in biology," Cassie finally began. "This guy Manny was being real rude to this kid Amal."

"Is he one of those Hispanics? We never had any kids like that in Minnesota. Hardly any."

"No, see, it's not just Hispanics, there was this other one—"

But they had arrived at Helen's door, and Helen threw down her book bag with a thud on the concrete step and began fishing for her key. Cassie had never been in Wakefield Gardens, and she was curious to see what the inside of the apartments would be like. Helen unlocked the blue door, which led to a concrete stairwell, where they walked up to the second floor. Here Helen took out a second key and unlocked a pink door. Opening it only a crack, she stuck her head in and called, "Yo, my name is Jo, I'm kinda slow. And somebody's with me, Mom."

"Oh, Ellie darling," answered a voice. "Well, just a minute." There were sounds of movement, while Helen did not move her body from the doorway. "Oh, my love, how wonderful, you brought a friend home."

Now Helen opened the door wider to reveal a thin woman in a pair of tight jeans and a silk shirt, with a cigarette in her hand and nails painted black. The nails were the first thing Cassie noticed.

"Come in, come in, darlings. Take your coats off, put your books down. Tell me all about it. Here, make yourselves comfortable." She sat down on a sofa herself, patting at her hair. "Do you smoke? Would you like a cigarette?"

Cassie laughed. "That's the second time I've been asked today. No, I definitely don't smoke."

"You're awfully young for such final decisions," Helen's mother suggested with a look that seemed to promise the universe.

"She doesn't smoke, okay?" said Helen. "This is Cassie, she lives in a house up the road. This is Meredith, my mother. You want something to eat? I'm starved."

"Oh yes, darling, that would be lovely." Meredith crossed her legs and looked happily at Cassie.

"Not you. Cassie. Are you hungry, Cass?"

"Me? Yeah, I guess so. It doesn't matter."

"Come here then."

"Sure." Cassie followed Helen into the kitchen. It was small, compared to the kitchen at home, but it had an adorable, homey look, with a window over the sink and clean new cabinets on the walls. Helen opened them, one at a time, with increasing impatience, and then tried the refrigerator. She took out a packet of American cheese slices.

"Hey, Mom, I thought you were going to go to the store today," she called out.

"Oh, darling, I've had so much to do."

"Did you call that office?"

There was silence from the other room, while Helen impatiently tossed the package of cheese from one hand to the other. "Did you call them?"

"I will tomorrow, darling."

Helen made a gruesome face at Cassie.

"What is it, the dentist or something?" murmured Cassie.

"No, she has to call places to get a job, but she never does it," said Helen, loud enough for her mother to hear. She led the way back to the little living room. "Can we have some money?" She held her hand out.

"All right, love, you can take Cassie down to the grocery store. And get something for supper, would you? Just some hot dogs or something."

"We had hot dogs last night." Helen stood in front of her mother, hand still waiting, stuffing a slice of the cheese into her mouth.

"Well, you think of something." She reached into a pocketbook on a table beside the sofa and handed Helen a ten, which Helen shoved into her pocket as she headed for the door. Looking back, Cassie was struck by the sight of Meredith, still sitting there, just smoking a cigarette.

"Doesn't your mother want a job?" Cassie asked, as they crossed a busy intersection toward the Safeway.

"Well, she does and she doesn't," Helen answered, and then was silent.

"What kind of a job?"

Helen looked away. "She thought she had like a job with the government, when we moved here. But it turned out, they didn't need her after all."

"How awful. So now she doesn't have anything?"

They were walking past a video store, where a group of young men, too old to be in high school, were just standing, watching whoever passed, watching the girls.

"She has welfare," Helen answered at last.

"Oh, that's too bad. I bet my mother could help her. That's what my mother does, she counsels people who are out of work. What kind of job was it that she was supposed to have? Has she got a degree or anything?"

Helen laughed, not very nicely, and Cassie realized she had made a mistake. "Anyway," she tried to correct, "my mother counsels all kinds of people. It doesn't matter what their skills or whatever are."

"That's good," said Helen, without any enthusiasm. They had reached the automatic door that swung open to receive them. Helen headed straight for the vegetable aisle and picked out a bag of oranges, a pound of carrots, and some potatoes.

"What will you have for dinner?" Cassie asked. "I never get to choose, this is fun."

"Never?"

"No, my mom is a big planner, she always has the week figured out in advance. If my dad ever calls and says he's staying late for a meeting she has a cow because it throws dinnertime off. Can't have overcooked chicken."

Helen looked at her and smiled ruefully now. "My best friend in Minnesota had a mother like that. She used to invite me over a lot. But I have to go home, pretty much. My mom gets . . . well. . . . See, she'll just watch TV all day, if she gets depressed. Right now she's scared about the jobs. I have to make sure she eats."

"I guess you really do a lot," said Cassie, thinking guiltily how she hated doing the breakfast dishes. "But will she be okay when she gets a job?"

"Who knows. Anyway, when she gives me money I have to buy, like, vegetables, otherwise we'd never eat any." Helen had also picked up a quart of milk and a loaf of bread, but she was contemplating the Little Debbie Snack Cakes.

"You better add that up," Cassie reminded her. "You've only got ten dollars."

"Yeah." Helen sighed, and put a hand on each item, rounding to the nearest half-dollar. It was enough. Helen packed the groceries into two plastic bags, handing one to Cassie as they left. Some guys from the high school were lounging outside the store; one was Ricardo.

Helen turned her shoulder past them, as if to indicate that she had no intention of recognizing them, and the boys likewise looked down at the pavement or out across the parking lot. Only Cassie stared momentarily at Ricardo, a word of greeting dying within her as she took in the scene. Ricardo's gaze lifted and swept past her. She smiled half-heartedly. "Hi," she said, but her voice squeaked.

Ricardo met her eyes for an instant, nodded, looked at Helen's turned shoulder, and mumbled to one of his buddies. Then the girls were past, walking down the sidewalk back toward the video store.

"You know that kid?" Helen asked in disapproval.

"Yeah, he's in my biology class, he—"

"He the one that almost got into a fight? You never finished telling me about that."

"No, not him, he's a good kid, actually, Helen, this is amazing, he said he liked my shirt. But really, what he was doing was, he didn't want Manny to be acting like that. See, this kid Manny was standing in the door, not letting anyone get past. And Amal, you know him? He's real, aggressive, I guess you could say. He was walking right up to him, with his fist like this."

"You have to steer clear of them," Helen advised. "Don't get involved in that stuff."

"Yeah, well I didn't mean to, but Ricardo was doing a good thing."

"Maybe, but don't go doing anything stupid like trying to be friends with him, okay? Promise me? I mean, maybe you knew a lot of different people from Panama and everything, but here it's a different story."

Cassie agreed out loud, stifling a doubt. What was a different story? She didn't tell Helen about meeting Ricardo later or how her heart flipped for a second; it was such a stupid reaction. It would probably never happen again.

At the corner, she realized it was time to go home, even though she had warned her mother this time that she would be late.

"Come to my place tomorrow?"

"Sure. Until I have to go home."

"Are you going to cook the potatoes, or is she?"

Helen laughed. "I make them the best, with melted cheese on top. Formidable. See you tomorrow."

"Sure."

Afterward, when Cassie remembered that they had never talked about her family, she didn't really mind. Helen's mother was so interesting, and there would be time later.

5

Helen did not come to visit the next day because she was not in school. Susan Carpenter took the opportunity to sit with Cassie at lunch. She reported all of her recent grades and her problems with getting her glasses fixed. Cassie didn't say much of anything. But just as Cassie was about to get up to dump her trash, Susan blurted out, "I guess you spend all your time with Helen now."

Cassie glanced nervously at Susan's wet eyes, behind the correctly adjusted glasses. "Sorry, Susan, but I guess I do."

Susan's mouth set in a firmer line. "Well, she's

real nice. She sure has a lot to talk about." Then abruptly Susan rose with her own trash, leaving Cassie alone.

In the evening Helen called with the good news that she had gone with her mother to a job interview, and her mother had done all right. She might even get the job, they would have to wait and see. The next day Helen and her mother were making curtains. Helen and her mother seemed to have all the fun, so Cassie kept going there to visit. At home everything was settled and none of the furniture ever moved. At the apartment, it was almost like camping out. Sometimes the three of them sat cross-legged on the floor together eating pickles and chips, or bagels and cream cheese. Once they all made cake together, and Meredith dotted their noses and chins with frosting. Meredith could do imitations of fat men giving job interviews, and then Helen would do Ms. Harkness being positive. They gave Cassie courage to do her own imitation of the leather jacket boys swaggering down the hall, while Meredith rolled over laughing. And then suddenly it was Thanksgiving.

"What will you and Meredith do?" Cassie asked.

Helen's mother had insisted Cassie call her by her first name.

"We always had this big ordeal at my cousin's, in Minnesota," Helen replied. "I guess I'll be glad not to go through that again."

"Why, was it bad?"

"It was okay, turkey and everything, only my Aunt Mildred was always nagging at my mother to *make* something of herself, and my mother always cried afterward."

Cassie had to go to an aunt and uncle's in Maryland, a couple without children that she hardly knew. She wondered about inviting Helen and Meredith along, but the more she tried to picture the event, the less likely it seemed. Her mother would have a fit if Meredith lit a cigarette, for starters, and everyone would probably stare at the black nail polish. Helen said they would be great, they would probably go out to dinner.

After Thanksgiving Cassie began to think it was past time for Helen to come to her house. Why hadn't it happened? Did Helen feel bad because she lived in a small apartment, while Cassie lived in a large house? Could Helen be shy about meeting her mother? It seemed to Cassie as if Helen could manage almost anything. Helen could call the building super and complain about a cracked window, she could read the want ads, she knew how to apply for food stamps. So why couldn't she visit Cassie?

When at last she did, the day was warm for December. The leaves from the oak trees, raked from all the yards into deep drifts along the street, lay waiting for the city to pick them up with its elephant trunk truck. Helen was talking about her aunt and uncle in Minnesota who had moved into a big new house and then immediately divorced. "My uncle had put the house in his own name and never told her, don't you think that's awful?"

"Yeah."

"So then, when it was time to get divorced, he wanted to stay in the house and for her to move out to this grungy little apartment. Men are so selfish."

"Yeah, I guess they are."

"But then, this judge, he decided to make my uncle pay this huge alimony, you know what that is?"

"Of course."

"That, plus child support, they had two children, really little, smaller than Jamie."

"They shouldn't divorce, if they have little children," said Cassie. "My parents would never do that. I think Jamie might even have been a mistake, but they would always stick with him, both of them. Besides, they get along."

They had reached Cassie's front door. She fished in her bag for the keys, waiting for some comment from Helen, who finally remarked, "I guess your folks make a lot of money, huh?"

Cassie looked at her carefully. "You should see some of the houses up the street," she said. "There's one with columns out front, I think the people have the idea it's a plantation."

"And little slaves, like, run and hang their coats up as soon as they get inside," Helen finished.

"They do have maids," Cassie added more seriously. "I've seen this car in the neighborhood that says Maids-in-Waiting. Isn't that a horrible name? How would you like to have to work cleaning houses and they called you maid-in-waiting?"

"But you guys don't have a maid, right?"

"Not us." Cassie led the way into the kitchen at the back of the house, letting her book bag fall somewhere near the closet door on her way, directing Helen to do the same. The sun was shining in the side kitchen window, warming up the white cabinets and the little round wood table where they ate family meals, still with a couple of breakfast bowls sitting on it. Cassie loaded them into the dishwasher while Helen sat in a kitchen chair, talking.

"Is that Jamie's bowl? Jeez, that's cute, let me see that. So he's three, he's eleven years younger than you are. I suppose your mother doesn't believe in abortion. My aunt in Minnesota was this real religious person, you wouldn't believe, she wouldn't even say it. She called it the A word. Did you know that babies actually suck their thumb when they're still inside?"

Cassie shook her head, taking Jamie's bowl back and letting water run over the cornflakes glued onto the rim. "You want something to eat? We could zap some popcorn."

"Great."

Cassie put a bag of popcorn in the microwave. Helen's eyes had fallen onto the little picture that hung over the sink, of Cassie's parents in their wedding clothes, kissing. "Your parents sure are good-looking," she said.

"Used to be. You want butter on the popcorn?"

"For sure."

"Let's take it to my room. You can see all my things."

It was good to get Helen into her room, Cassie realized, watching her friend sprawled over her bed. Cassie showed her the treasures of her travels, the beautiful woven basket from Panama, the yearbook from Germany that showed her in braces, her old stuffed animals.

"You saved all this stuff?" Helen asked.

"My mom saves it. You'd think with all this moving we'd throw everything out, but Mom's a big saver." Cassie imitated her mother's sentimental voice. "Oh, sweetheart, not lamby, you wouldn't throw away lamby."

Helen laughed appreciatively. "That's not Meredith, Meredith is like, oh my gaaaaaad, you still got daaaaaalls in your room." Helen held an invisible cigarette exactly the way her mother did.

"Is that what she says? She made you throw them out?"

"No, she didn't make me, I threw them out myself. Get rid of the ratty old things. Make a little space or something."

The door opened downstairs, and Jamie's happy little voice came piping upward, along with Cassie's mother's quieter tones.

"Cassie's home today."

Murmur, murmur.

"C'mon, let's go down and meet them," Cassie said. "Remember, I've still got to know what you think about my mom."

Cassie's mother and Helen shook hands politely and said their how-do-you-do's, while Jamie put his finger in his nose, watching Helen suspiciously.

"How about if we take him for a walk?" Cassie volunteered. "Wonderful," said her mother. "It's a lovely day. You won't even need your winter coats. Don't go too far, you big girls, remember his legs are little."

Jamie was quieter than usual and made sure that Cassie always came between Helen and himself.

"So, this is what you do if you go home in the afternoon?" Helen started. "You always have to take him for a walk?"

"Not always."

"Is he short for his age, or what? How old did you say he is?"

"He's three, almost four. No, he's not short. He's normal."

"My cousin had this kid, out in Minnesota, who was missing some hormone, and he didn't grow. You should have seen him, what a little freak. He had this, like, huge head, and funny-looking little body. So they found this doctor that gave him shots every day, at the hospital. My cousin is, like, hey, I'm practically living at this hospital."

"Ouch, Jamie, quit holding my hand so tight. I didn't know you were so strong. C'mon, let's look for pretty bottle caps, just like Ernie. You pick out the best one and bring it back to show Mom."

But Jamie would not let go, so Cassie had to change the subject. "See this house? This is the one

I was telling you about. Isn't it ugly? I mean, who do they think they are?"

"Yeah, really. I'm glad your house isn't like that. Your mom, too. She's okay."

"Do you think so?" Cassie wasn't sure whether she was glad or disappointed, but just then Jamie did let go of her hand to scoot after a bottle cap.

"Look, Cassie, I found one."

"Good for you, Jamie. It says Sprite, right there. See the *S*?"

Cassie missed half of what Helen was saying. ". . . what she would think about *my* mother."

"Do you remember, back when we first met, and I bought that shirt, and I said my mother didn't like it? Yes, yes, Jamie, I see, *two* more."

"Hey, Jamie," Helen addressed him for the first time. "I saw a whole pile of them, way back at the beginning of the block."

Jamie stared at Helen with distrust, and then looked at Cassie. "She's kidding," said Cassie, avoiding Helen's look. "She didn't really." Jamie gripped her hand again.

"Did I tell you what Sharon said?" Helen continued. "About my jeans? I mean, what business is it of *hers*."

"We have to start home," said Cassie, only half reluctantly. "This is as far as he goes."

Just before dinner, after Helen had gone home and the family was gathered, Cassie made an announcement that had been building in her, she now believed, for weeks.

She blurted it right out. "It's not fair to make me take Jamie for walks after school."

Neither parent said anything for a moment, and only Jamie looked at her, with big eyes that made her squirm.

"Well, I'm fourteen, I have my own life. He's not my kid, he's your kid. And I have lots of things to do. I mean, I have, like, homework, I have shopping, I need time to be with my friends, okay?"

She saw her parents exchange a look, but she couldn't see closely enough to decide what it meant. Then her father announced, pompously, "Everyone in a family contributes in some way. Your mother has a long day at work, and she deserves a break in the afternoon."

"Well, I have a long day, too. What about my break?" Cassie was pleased with the energy of her own defense. She was getting sure of herself; it must be because of Helen.

"It's all right," her mother replied gently. "I'll take care of Jamie. Maybe we could think of some other way for you to contribute." They flashed their eye signals again.

"Like what?" Cassie asked suspiciously.

"Would you like to do the dinner dishes?" her father asked.

"Every day?" Cassie looked around the kitchen, dismayed. Her mother was a good cook, but she used a lot of dishes. "I already do breakfast. You always say I put them in the dishwasher wrong."

"How about three days a week," her mother suggested mildly. "And we'll show you once more about the dishwasher and then not bother you."

"I don't think that's much work for a fourteen-year-old to be doing," her father objected. "What about the laundry? Can't she run a washing machine?"

"All right," her mother agreed. "You do the

dishes on Wednesday, Friday, and Sunday, and take care of your own laundry. Is it a deal?" She looked Cassie in the eye for the first time.

"All right." Today was Tuesday; no dishes. That was a relief, anyway. So as soon as dinner was over, Cassie could go to the upstairs phone and call Helen and tell her about the deal. "Great news. We don't have to worry about Jamie anymore." That's what she would say.

6

XXX

The he weather turned cold, but there was no snow. The school held a Christmas dance—or a "winter holiday" dance, as Helen reminded Cassie with a laugh. They didn't even consider going. Meredith's family sent her money to travel home for the holiday, so Cassie had a lonely time around Christmas, but she bought Helen a beautiful edition of Emily Dickinson's poetry, and Helen sent her a handmade card and a picture of their whole tribe around a perfectly set table with a turkey in the middle. She wrote that she was gladder than ever that she and

Meredith had left Minnesota, and she couldn't wait to see Cassie again.

After school resumed, Cassie noticed signs for a special ninth-grade-only dance, for the third Friday in January. She mentioned it one afternoon at Meredith's. "Grace asked me if I was going," she added.

"Grace is going around with that basketball player. Have you seen how tall he is? And skinny? I saw him in his basketball shorts one time, and his knees are the widest part of his legs."

"She said people aren't going with dates, they're just going. Or girls are going together, and stuff."

Helen laughed. "You trying to fix me up with Grace? No *thank* you, sweetheart."

But Meredith turned suddenly away from her TV show. "Don't be silly, darlings. Of course you should go."

"Meredith! Dances are so conventional. You want us to turn all boring on you?"

"But you might like it, Helen. And if you don't like it, you can tell me funny stories about it."

Gradually, it became settled that they would go.

They spoke of it often, during the week before, though always mockingly, assuring each other that a dance was of no importance.

"Oh Lordy, how can I ever decide what to *wear*."

"And I don't even have time to get my hair done!"

Still, Cassie discovered that she was pleased, and she was sure that her parents would be pleased, too. Her mother had been criticizing her social life recently.

"Cassie, I don't like to see you spending so much time with just one person. How about joining in some of the social activities at the school? My school used to have such nice plays and clubs and dances and games, and I know all kinds of things are going on."

To which Cassie would reply, "That's nice, I'm glad you had a good time, but I'm not you, remember?" She felt the sting in her mother's words, the idea that she was still somehow not a social success. So it would be good to announce that she was going to a school dance. She waited until her father would be there, too, which might have been a mistake.

"Some guy ask you, Cassie?" he said, with too much hope in his voice. So he thought she was a flop, too.

"No, Dad, girls don't have to wait for guys anymore. I'm going with Helen."

"I see." He was playing with Jamie at the same time, and he allowed himself to be distracted for a few minutes, making truck gearshifting noises.

"Just Helen?" her mother asked, in a tone not nearly pleased enough.

"Yeah, Mom, just Helen. Why, how many people should I go with? You afraid we'll get lost or something?"

"Don't start twisting my words. You're getting rather difficult to get along with, Cassandra Winn. Actually I was thinking about Susan Carpenter. You haven't even returned her phone calls lately, and I think she's given up trying. It's awfully rude of you. And I don't see why you two soul mates couldn't invite her along, too."

Cassie's stomach lurched at the very suggestion, in part because of the twinge of guilt she felt. She had definitely discouraged Susan; but then, what could a person do? "Look, Mom," she said angrily,

"I'm not required to be friends with anybody who just hangs on to me, okay? I don't like Susan Carpenter. Will you get that through your head?"

"This is the first time I've ever heard that one. I think maybe it's your friend Helen who doesn't like Susan, am I right?"

"No, you are *not* right, I never have liked Susan, and you can't keep me from making the friends that I like."

"I can keep you from being rude to someone who really tried to welcome you to a new school. You can't just drop her, Cassie. She's a person, not an old Barbie doll. So if you want permission to go to the dance, you just ask Susan to come along."

"Mom!" Cassie was outraged. "Dad, are you going to let her do this?"

"Do what?"

"Come on, Dad, you heard everything. Quit pretending."

"Well, what difference does it make, if you go with one girl or two? If you were going with a boy, I'd think it was kind of outrageous."

Cassie slammed out of the kitchen and wouldn't eat dinner that night, but her parents remained firm, and Helen showed a curious disinterest. "Sure, ask the little creep," she said. "We can drop her in a hurry."

So Cassie told Susan that she and Helen were going to the dance, and that Susan could come along if she wanted to. Susan was extremely grateful, and asked three times what time Cassie's father would pick her up, because she didn't want to make them wait. Cassie's mother seemed to be truly pleased, and gave Cassie an extra ten dollars. Even Cassie began to feel that she had done something generous. Looking at herself, the night of the dance, in her white shirt, and a new pair of tight jeans, with her shoulder-length brown hair freshly combed, she saw a face in the mirror that she could like. She was not beautiful, in fact she was not even as good-looking as Susan, but she was good-looking enough. She looked, she thought, like a nice person, like someone who had friends, someone you might want to talk to.

Helen walked up to her house. She had put on makeup and she was wearing a very short, very tight skirt that Cassie's mother obviously disapproved of.

"You didn't tell me you were going to wear that,"

Cassie scolded her, lightly, when her mother was out of the room.

Helen waved her hand, as if it were nothing. "My mom made me do it. This is her idea of how to dress."

Cassie laughed. "Moms. Contemptible lunatics."

"Do I look that bad?"

"No, you look cool. Come on, let's go."

"What time are you picking them up, Teddy?" called Cassie's mother from the kitchen.

"We said eleven. Is that okay?" he asked the girls.

Helen shrugged her agreement, and Cassie said, "Sure, that's fine. Don't worry, we'll look for you right outside. You know where the dance is, in the cafeteria? We'll look for you right outside that door, by the student parking lot."

They picked up Susan, who was standing at her door waiting, and who squeezed herself into the backseat rather than get in front with Cassie's father. But Cassie spoke to her politely, until they were all let out at the door. "Right here then, at eleven. Have a good time, girls," he said, and they were rid of him.

The cafeteria had not been decorated, and the

band was only a bunch of kids from school. Those were all the first impressions Cassie had, before Grace came up and stood beside her.

"Hi," said Grace. "I didn't know you were coming."

"Oh, hi. I guess we just decided at the last minute."

"I haven't seen you in a long time. I have basketball practice just about every afternoon now."

"I hear you're doing pretty well." Cassie didn't know anything about the basketball team, but it seemed like a reasonable thing to say. She was aware of Susan and Helen both standing there, as if they were using her as a shield between themselves and the rest of the kids.

"Yeah, we won against Alexandria, that was pretty good. But we lost to Falls Church. I never met your new friend."

"Oh." Cassie felt slightly awkward, but she made the introduction, and she managed to add, "And this is Susan Carpenter, I guess you know her already."

"Sure. Hi, Susan. Well listen, let's go get something to drink."

So now there were four of them. Cassie had a wonderful rising sensation that this was going to be a success. Here she was, with *three* friends, walking through clumps of kids, feeling at home, feeling that she belonged here. She asked Grace what position she played, and decided that she might want to go to a basketball game sometime—with Helen, and maybe even Susan.

At a long table set up along one side of the cafeteria, several parents and a few teachers were serving punch. Mr. McCutcheon was there.

"Here come some of my very own pupils," he said, with a bow that tickled Cassie.

"Need any metaphors today, Mr. McCutcheon?" Helen asked.

"I search for an apt comparison for four such lovely ladies," he replied gallantly, with a wink. "And here comes Miss Sharon."

Sharon almost yanked her punch out of his hand, turning enthusiastically to Cassie. "So, you came to the dance. You look good. Is that a new shirt?"

"No, I bought it last fall."

"I picked it out for her," said Helen.

"You did not. I found it myself."

"How do you like my earrings?" Sharon asked. "You can tell the truth, they belong to my sister."

The earrings were heavy, long, and ugly to Cassie's eye, full of artificial sparkle. "They're okay," she said hesitantly.

But Helen laughed. "Cassie has better earrings than that," she said. "Hey, Cass, you should have worn your dad's earrings."

"Cassie's dad has earrings?" Sharon asked, and they all began to laugh.

Somewhere in there, Cassie could never remember exactly where, Steve from Latin class sidled in among them. Sharon seemed to know him pretty well. "So, Steve, I hear your brother got a car."

"Yeah, but he has to pay the insurance himself, and he won't let me drive it."

"You're not old enough, anyway," Sharon reminded him.

"Well, yeah, but just around the driveway and stuff." Steve looked at Cassie and Helen carefully. "Where'd you go to elementary school?" he asked.

"None around here," Cassie answered. "Helen's from Minnesota, I'm from all over."

"So you're both new in town?"

"I'm newer than she is," said Helen, and stuck out her tongue.

He didn't seem to like that, and turned his body more toward Cassie. "Aren't you taking Latin?"

"Sure, I'm in your class. You do some real good translations."

Steve looked pleased. "What'd you get on the last quiz?"

"A."

"She always gets As," said Sharon, and somewhere in the background, Susan made quiet agreeing noises.

"Why don't you dance with her?" suggested Sharon. People were dancing now, a few of them, and the band was nearly drowning out conversation, anyway.

Cassie never knew why Sharon said that to Steve, but Steve looked almost obedient as he grabbed her hand and led her toward an open area. Cassie glanced once over her shoulder, throwing an apologetic smile at Helen, and then she tried to observe what the other dancers were actually doing. It looked easy enough, so when

Steve squared off opposite her, Cassie began to dance.

She forgot to worry about not knowing how to dance; the music seemed to move her body for her. After a few minutes she glanced around. People were doing different things, dancing with their arms or their hips or their feet, but she saw Steve grinning at her, so she figured she was all right. When the music stopped momentarily, Cassie and Steve just stood there, smiling. Then it began again, faster, better, and Cassie began to dance once more. This is what it feels like to be happy, she said to herself.

Someone touched her shoulder; it was Sharon, dancing beside her. Sharon grabbed Cassie's hand, and the two of them whirled around together, like old sixties dancing, grinning in each other's faces. Sharon liked her, then. Lots of people liked her; the dancers began to stamp in unison, and Cassie stamped with them, laughing at Steve, laughing at Sharon, feeling, wonderfully, like a part of the whole room, the whole roomful of people all of whom liked her.

The music slowed and came to a stop. Cassie realized that she was a little dizzy; faces opposite to her whirled and then steadied. She looked for Helen, but did not see her. Steve wandered away, but another boy took his place. Cassie did not even know his name, but it didn't matter; when the music started again, she danced.

She must have been dancing for an hour before she decided she ought to sit down for a few minutes. She looked at the people around her and was not even sure which one she was dancing with, so without saying anything she walked toward the refreshments again, needing punch. But there was a line, so she went out into the hall for a water fountain. She drank for a long time, letting the cooler air of the hall caress her neck and shoulders and armpits. Her shirt had damp underarm spots, in spite of deodorant.

When she reentered the room, she looked more carefully for Helen, but could not see her anywhere. She saw Susan, sitting by herself on a metal folding chair on the far wall, but she did not move in that direction. And then right next to her she saw Manny and Ricardo, and another one of their crowd. She stood still. They didn't appear to see her. They did not have their leather jackets on; they were dressed in white shirts with collars and khakis with sharp creases down the front. Ricardo's hair fell just over his collar, soft and clean-looking.

Then Manny saw her, and spoke to her. "Hey, babe, you been doing some dancin'."

Cassie froze. Had her dancing stood out in some way, to make her ridiculous? She clamped her elbows against her ribs, the damp spots cold now. She nodded at him vaguely, and took a step away, toward the lines at the punch table.

Ricardo came right behind her. "You're a good dancer," he said, no irony in his voice.

"Thank you."

"It's a long line for punch."

"Yes. But I'm very thirsty."

"Yeah." He stood there with her, clearly as unsure what to say as she was herself.

"Were you there when Mr. Raffensberger tried to dissect the frog?" she asked.

"Yeah, that was too bad. The kids don't treat him right."

"He's pretty old, for a teacher. And maybe he never was that good. He doesn't even know who I am, sometimes he calls me Susan."

"That's what you think? You think he's a bad teacher?"

"Sure, I think so. Don't you?"

"Yeah, but I didn't think you would ever say something like that."

How awkward this conversation was, compared to talking with Helen! Cassie almost wished he would go away now. It was nice that he seemed to like her and that he didn't always stick with the same crowd, but she felt how little they knew about each other.

"Do you live in Wakefield Gardens?" she tried.

"No, not there. The one next to it."

Now what? "Helen lives in Wakefield Gardens."

They reached the end of the punch line at last, and parted as if they were opposing magnets. Cassie wandered vaguely toward Susan.

"Have you seen Helen?" she asked when she got there. The room was crowded now, and she might easily have missed her.

"No, not for a while. I saw you dancing. You were great," Susan told her.

"Thanks."

"It's almost eleven. Your father said he'd meet

us at eleven. Maybe we should start over that way."

Cassie looked at her watch. It really was about ten till eleven. The time had seemed fast and wonderful, and she half wanted to be late for her father, just to plague him, just to show him how popular she was. "He won't care if we're a few minutes late. Anyway, I've got to find Helen. Where'd you last see her?"

"With some boys."

"Which boys?"

Susan shrugged. "I don't know them. Just some boys. Maybe we should wait for your father without her."

"Without her! What are you talking about? Why would we leave without her? How would she get home?"

Susan looked unhappy. "Maybe they have cars."

"Helen's not going to drive home with some boy. Not without even telling us. She's probably just waiting for us somewhere."

Leaving Susan watching worriedly at the door, Cassie made the whole round of the room, slowly. She saw Grace and Sharon leave, together, toward a waiting car. She saw Mr. McCutcheon packing up a punch bowl, joking with another teacher, looking tired. She saw Steve dancing with someone she didn't know, one of the last couples. But no Helen.

She saw Ricardo and Manny, and steered around them, but Ricardo place himself in her path. "You looking for your friend?"

Cassie nodded.

"She's out in the parking lot."

Cassie thanked him. But when she went to the door and scanned the parking lot, she still could not see her. Susan came up beside her and repeated her theory. "I think we should go home without her."

"Tell you what, Susan. You go search the girls' room, maybe she's in there. And after that, maybe look around the school. I'll keep watch here for a while."

Susan was looking more and more unhappy. "She's not in the girls' room," she said.

"How do you know? Have you seen her, or what?"

"Well, I guess I saw her go outside."

"Well, why didn't you say so?" Susan was so exasperating. "You go look in the girls' room anyway, in case you're wrong. And I'll search the parking lot."

Susan obediently turned away, and Cassie went out into the cold. The lot was crowded, too small for all the parents' cars that were arriving and turning around, but Cassie made her way among them to the far end, where the kids who could drive sometimes parked their cars. She was alone out here and felt creepy; there was a wind and she had left her coat inside. She folded her arms across herself, tightly, walking past the empty cars. She got to the end of the row and came back. And then she saw what she'd half anticipated, Helen's head. And a guy in there, too, in the backseat.

While Cassie hesitated, they began kissing. Peering around to make sure no one was close, Cassie said Helen's name, then said it louder. They were still kissing. She yelled out loud, once. Then they stopped kissing, but they still didn't act as if they had heard her. She saw her father's car, which had finally made its way through the crowd and up to the cafeteria door, and she heard its three impatient beeps.

She took a step closer to the car and rapped on the window.

The boy rolled the window down, slowly, not taking his arm from around the back of Helen's neck. "Whatd'ya want, nerd?" he drawled.

"Hey, shut up, that's my friend," said Helen, and then began to laugh.

"You got quite a parade of nerdy friends," he said rudely, looking straight at Cassie. "They all like to watch, or what?"

"It's after eleven, Helen," said Cassie. She could not keep the anger out of her voice. "My father's over there honking."

"Oh." Helen shook her head and moved herself away from the boy. "Oh yeah."

"Forget it, babe. I'll give you a ride home."

Helen hesitated. Cassie could smell beer in the car, and realized that she had no idea how much the boy had drunk, or whether Helen had drunk some, too, and anyway, how much was too much.

"You better come home with us," said Cassie firmly.

"Just because I'm having the good time," said

Helen with some spite. "First you had the good time, now what about me?"

"All right. I'm sorry I danced so much. But, Helen, you *have* to come home with us. What would I tell my dad?"

Helen giggled. "I don't know, kid, what *would* you tell him?"

She must be drunk. *"Helen!"*

"Yeah," Helen agreed, slowly. "Right." She opened the door and got out, smoothing her skirt down over her legs. "See ya later," she said carelessly to the boy, and walked toward the cafeteria, letting Cassie follow.

"What did you do that for?" Cassie complained. "You made us late, my father's going to be mad." But even as she said it, she knew that her question was stupid. What does anybody do that for? Helen had already done similar things in Minnesota. But Cassie was surprised when Helen had a ready answer.

"So who left who, anyway? What was I supposed to do, stand around watching you all night?"

"Oh." Cassie saw that she might apologize, but then she wasn't sure about it. Weren't you supposed to dance, at a dance? She got nowhere with that thought, because her father had seen them.

"Hey, Cassie, what are you doing over there? Hurry up, it's almost twenty minutes after, they're turning the lights out."

"Sorry, Dad, we just had to say good-night to some people."

"Okay, get in, let's go. Where's Susan?"

Where *was* Susan? Cassie saw that he was right about the cafeteria lights; only a security light was left on, and the teachers were leaving.

"Gosh, I don't know."

"What do you mean, you don't know?" He turned around to look at them.

"She told me she was getting a ride home with someone else," said Helen.

"What? She did? When did she tell you that?"

"When she was out there spying on me. She said she didn't feel too well and she was going to get a ride home with someone. Named Connie, I think."

"But I talked to her after that. She didn't say anything about getting a ride."

"Well, I can't help that." Helen got into the car and slammed the door.

"Well, I wish someone would let me in on the arrangements." Cassie's father restarted his engine and the headlights shone on the brick wall of the school and the closed door. Cassie swallowed hard. Anyway, Susan wasn't there. And yet, it was just possible that she had talked to Connie about getting a ride home, maybe while Cassie was dancing. And then, when Cassie had disappeared into the parking lot, and Susan would be so worried about being late, sure, she could have figured Cassie and Helen had both driven away with the boys, and she should get another ride home. It sort of made sense.

They dropped Helen at her apartment with a simple good-night, Cassie's father waiting until she was inside the blue door before he left, and then they were met at their own door by her mother.

"Oh, thank goodness you're here, Susan's mother has been calling. It took you a long time to pick them up."

Teddy stopped right where he was on the walk. "Susan's not home?"

"Well no, didn't you just drop her?"

He was furious. He actually grabbed Cassie by

the scruff of the neck and shook her lightly. "So where in God's name did you leave her?" he roared.

Scared, Cassie told how Helen had been difficult to find and how she had sent Susan to look for Helen. She fibbed about what happened in the parking lot and how probably Susan knew about it.

Steaming, Cassie's father marched her back to the car by an elbow and planted her in the front seat. They drove back to the school, empty and dark now, the security light making one dim pool outside the door. And there was Susan, huddled against the wall, crying.

She tried to stop, but couldn't. "I thought you f-f-forgot me," she said. "When I came out from the girls' room, everybody was gone. I came out into the parking lot and it was em-em-empty"—she blew her nose very correctly into a tissue—"and then the door had locked behind me, so I couldn't get back in to call somebody. Here, Cassie, you left your coat."

All the way home, Cassie's father comforted Susan with explanations of how it happened, including Cassie's carelessness, as he called it. Susan said it was perfectly all right, she understood completely how it had happened, and she was just being a baby about it. At Susan's house he insisted on going in to make his own apologies to Susan's mother. Cassie stayed in the car, pulling her coat around herself, angry. Everybody was being bad to her. It was the first time she had really had a good time, and look what happened. Everybody just dumped on her. And Helen worst of all.

7

XXX

On Monday morning Cassie wore one of the old stripy turtlenecks and did not look up when Helen came bouncing into English, slapping her books onto the desk, greeting Sharon and Rebecca and even Miguel, who didn't answer, knowing she was putting on an act.

"Hey, Cass," she whispered. "Guess what?" Mr. McCutcheon was doing grammar today, a prospect that made Cassie's spirits sink even lower, but she pretended to be paying great attention, and did not answer Helen. But that didn't dampen Helen, either.

"My mother got a job," she whispered again.

Cassie couldn't help reacting this time, as her mind flew over all the kinds of difference that would make. "Really?"

"She's a receptionist, at this big, like, company. She gets eighteen thousand a year. Isn't that formidable?"

Cassie nodded, happy for Helen in spite of her anger. Helen had not had any new clothes since she got here, and she never suggested that they go to the movies or even back to Roy's. Maybe these things made you bad-tempered after a while. Still, that was no reason for Helen to get Cassie in trouble with her father. Cassie turned away and raised her hand, and then didn't know what the question was when Mr. McCutcheon called on her.

But when the bell rang, Cassie packed her books slowly, unwilling to ignore Helen entirely. She wanted to tell Helen exactly what had happened after they dropped her off, and just how angry her father had been. But Helen complimented Rebecca on her sweater, and then she was gone.

They didn't speak for the rest of that week, until Cassie felt as lonely as she had felt in September, or lonelier, in a way, because there sat Helen, not her friend. A whole weekend of Jamie and parents passed. On Monday, at lunch, Cassie hunched her shoulders, took her tray to their usual table, and said stiffly, "I'm glad your mother got a job."

Helen brightened up immediately. She was full of details about the job, which was perfect for her mother because the chief responsibility was to be charming to clients. "And she's, like, now I can write home and really tell them something. And she goes, let's get you something nice, for a treat. Hey, see that guy over there? That's the one."

Cassie was caught off guard. "One what?"

Helen laughed. "One guy. The guy in the parking lot."

"Oh."

Cassie couldn't tell which one of a whole table of guys Helen meant, because they all looked nearly the same to her; they were white, they wore jeans and T-shirts with the names of musical groups or auto parts stores on them, and they roved together in bands in the hallways. "What's his name?" Cassie asked, trying to like them.

"Hugh. Isn't that contemptible? I'm surprised he admits it."

"Is he nice, or what?"

"He's okay."

"Helen, why'd you do that on Friday night?"

"It wasn't that much, really. I mean we were just kissing, not, like, you know. I don't have AIDS, okay?"

"That's not what I mean. You told us Susan got a ride home, but she didn't. You knew she didn't. Why?"

Helen turned her head so that Cassie could only see a profile, with a mouth set in objection.

"You should have seen my dad, Helen. He was furious. I mean, he *shook* me. We had to go back for her. She was locked out of the school, and she was crying."

At the mention of crying, Helen turned slowly back, and then started to smile. "Crying? Actually crying? What a little dweeb. Isn't that exactly what you'd expect?" Helen laughed.

Cassie started to laugh, too. It was true, Susan was absurd. Crying, think of it. "But, Helen," she said more softly. "Why *did* you say that about Susan getting a ride?"

"Why did I?" Helen roused up with a new energy. "I'll tell you why I did. The little dweeb came out there in the parking lot, spying on me."

"She was probably worried about getting home."

"She was *spying* on me. She was going to spread rumors all over school. Standing there watching the whole thing, the little *voyeur*."

Cassie thought back. It was true, Susan had seemed to know where Helen was.

"So then she knocks on the window, and she's, like, I'm gonna tell Cassie to go home without you. The nerve. I guess I paid *her* back." Helen shook her straggly hair.

It did seem understandable, the way Helen told it, and Cassie hardly knew what she felt now. "My dad was real mad at me," she repeated, more gently.

Now Helen looked straight at her, with her blue eyes. "I'm sorry," she said sincerely. "I guess I didn't think about that part."

"Were you mad at me, too?"

"Maybe a little." Helen put her hand on Cassie's shoulder. "I thought we were gonna, you know, hang out together. And then you went off dancing with this nothing, this little jerk. And you didn't come back."

"I'm sorry, Helen." Now Cassie put both hands on Helen's shoulders, and they both began to laugh.

"Hey, lovebirds, lunch is over," Sharon called at them, passing with a tray of trash. That made them both laugh harder.

On Tuesday morning Helen paid more attention in English but she passed a card to Cassie. It had a picture of two toddlers kissing, and inside another Emily Dickinson poem, copied out with Helen's purple pen.

The Soul selects her own Society—
Then—shuts the Door—
To her divine Majority—
Present no more—

. . . . .

I've known her—from an ample nation—
Choose One—
Then—close the Valves of her attention—
Like Stone—

The last lines were squeezed into tiny print on the back of the card, but Cassie was able to make them out. She kept reading the poem over and over, smiling and almost crying.

Report cards were given out that Friday. It was the end of the second marking period, but Cassie had forgotten all about it. Her excellent reports were such a routine that even her parents scarcely paid any attention to them, beyond a conventional pat on the back. Grades weren't all that important to her parents, Cassie told herself. They really didn't pay that much attention to what happened to her in school.

What happened was only that Cassie got a C in math, a C in keyboarding, and a B in English. Mr. McCutcheon also added a note explaining that Cassie's behavior in class was not what it used to be. She still got As in biology and Latin; so what's the big deal, as she said to herself while walking home. Helen was not there to agree with her because she had gone to see a teacher to complain. Susan Carpenter had all As again; they both regularly called her "the little dweeb."

That afternoon Cassie did some of everyone's

laundry and volunteered to take Jamie for a walk, so naturally she didn't think to show them her report card until after her father had had his glass of wine, and just minutes before dinner went on the table.

"Ah, report card time again," said Cassie's father, without removing the card from the manila envelope. "You know, Cass, now that you're in ninth grade, we have to take this grade business more seriously."

"Why?" asked Cassie, getting out the milk for Jamie.

"Because these are the grades that colleges pay attention to." The card slid out of the envelope, and his cheerful, expectant look changed a shade. Cassie sat down at the table. Her mother set a salad on the table beside the pot of stew and sat down herself.

Without a word, her father handed the card to his wife and began to serve the stew. The pot smelled good. Chunks of onion, carrot, and turnip came out with the meat, all covered in gravy.

"Not that!" screamed Jamie, pointing at the vegetables in his little Peter Rabbit plate.

"Just give him carrots," said her mother, reaching behind her to set the report card on the kitchen counter.

"You like all these frightening vegetables, Cassie?" asked her father.

"Sure, give me heaps. Thank you."

Everyone began to eat. The forks clinked, and Jamie hummed while he chewed, tunelessly, but then more purposefully, until he finally settled on "Rubber Duckie" and began to form the words.

"Don't sing with your mouth full," said Cassie irritably. He stopped for a full second looking at her, his mouth open and full of masticated carrot. Then he closed and began humming again.

"What happened in math?" her mother asked finally. She sounded self-conscious; Cassie could tell she was making an effort to be reasonable.

"Not that much, really," Cassie replied. "The teacher is awful. We started trig and he can't explain it. I can't even do the homework. Everybody's doing bad."

"Is that right," said her father drily, not as a question.

"Except a couple of geeky mathematical geniuses, okay?" Cassie added. And more emphatically, "They're all guys."

"And the keyboarding?" her mother asked.

"Oh, Mom, it's just this dumb class, it's not one of the real courses you have to take. I can type, she just makes us do these incredibly stupid exercises."

"And English?" said her father.

"Look, what is this, the Spanish Inquisition? I got a B in English, that's a good grade, okay? I have a B average. A lot of parents would kill for a B average." But looking at their faces, Cassie realized she was not having the desired effect.

After a minute her mother asked, "Which of these classes is Helen in?"

Cassie jumped, inwardly. "What's that got to do with anything?"

"I don't know, that's what I'm trying to find out. Helen has English with you, doesn't she? Isn't that what this behavior note is about?"

"Yes, Helen has English with me, and I have no idea what this behavior note is about."

"And math?" her mother persisted.

"Yes, Helen's in math."

"And keyboarding?"

"Yes, all right already, Helen's in keyboarding."

"But she's not in Latin, you told me that. How about biology?"

This was looking really bad. Cassie thought about lying, but it would be too easy for her parents to find out. Guidance counselors would tell them in a minute. "She's not in biology." She thought about trying to explain away her A in biology as the meaningless thing it was, but that didn't quite make sense.

"So, it looks like a pattern," said her father. "What do we do?" He was looking at her mother.

"Well," she began reasonably, "I don't think we should blow this out of proportion. I know Cassie can bring these grades up in the next marking period. Maybe all we need is a little more regular homework time."

"We," Cassie mocked her.

"Yes, we," said her father. He was seriously cross. "You and I are going to do math homework together, every night. I can explain trigonometry."

"And I think," said her mother judiciously, "maybe you should give up the afternoon visits to Helen for a while."

"Oh, Mom!" Cassie suddenly felt like bursting into tears. "Mom, this is ridiculous, okay? You have this bad influence idea, off of TV or something. What do you think she does, pushes drugs and dirty needles? Get a little perspective." She stopped, hearing herself. What was happening? Was this herself, Cassandra Winn, fighting with her parents over a bad report card, over supposedly bad friends? She was like a real American teenager. Not like. Was. She had been suppressing tears, and now she was suppressing a smile.

Her mother got up from the table, clearing away dishes, and now her father's tone got even heavier. "We're not going to argue about this, Cassandra. No visits to Helen for a month, and then we'll see how the grades are doing. I'll look over the trig with you in the evening. And in the meantime, it's your dishes night." He got up and carried his dish to the sink.

"Ice cream," said Jamie.

"Maybe later, boy, after your bath."

Cassie sulked. Her smile had vanished as airily as it had come. She wanted to call Helen but she didn't want to be overheard, and she wanted, wildly, to be outrageous. "Dad," she called after him as he led Jamie away, "can I have a phone in my room?"

"No, you can't," he answered, without turning around, and the answer satisfied Cassie, like picking at a sore hangnail.

She couldn't wait until her parents went out for their errands on Saturday morning, so she could call Helen in privacy. Helen entered into the matter with feeling. She was indignant at the injustice of being considered a cause of Cassie's grades slipping. "Do they think I'm dumb or something? Why do they think that?"

"Who knows. They never asked me what you got. All they did was ask which classes we have together, and that was that, case closed. By the way, what'd you get in English?"

"A."

"You did? The rotten creep! Did you get a little note about misbehavior in class?"

"Yeah, I got that part. I guess passing poems to each other is pretty contemptible."

"Contemptible." Cassie laughed away her jealousy over the grade. "I love your words."

By Monday morning Helen had a plan. "You know what we should do, Cass? Since they won't let us spend any time together? We should skip school."

"Seriously?"

"What time do we get together, anyway? Two minutes at lockers before class. Three minutes between classes, and you have to run to the other end of the building. Twenty minutes for lunch, and you spend half of it in line, you jerk, instead of bringing your lunch. I'd like to see their faces if they weren't allowed to talk to anyone at work."

"But what would we do?"

"Well, we could, like, take a bus downtown."

"We could go to a museum or something."

Helen rolled her eyes. "Sure, all right. I've never been to that big one, what do they call it, the Smithsonian. But I'm warning you, I'm not too patient with dinosaurs."

Cassie considered carefully. "We could be back by the end of school. And we could just forge the notes about why we were absent."

"Half the time they forget to collect them, anyway."

Cassie knew this was true. She remembered an old daydream, from her lonely time, about going into the city with a friend. It could be true, it could be true now. "Do the Metrobus drivers ask you anything?" She had only been to the city by car.

"Never. My mom and I went in, bunches of times, before she got her job."

"But you were with your mother."

"Don't be crazy, okay? They're just bus drivers, they don't care."

8

After enduring nearly an hour of trigonometry with her father, Cassie went up to her room and lay crosswise over the bed. She looked at the bedraggled row of stuffed animals, their glassy eyes at odd angles, their noses worn from lying upside down on the floor, their fur matted and dirty. She looked at the beautiful woven basket from Panama. She looked at her white ruffled shirt, where it hung always on the hook on the back of her door, so she could see it. It wasn't so new anymore; it looked laundered rather than crisp.

Would she, Cassie, really skip school? Would she go downtown without her parents' permission?

Cassie turned over onto her back, thinking about Ricardo's face. His skin was the color of cider, with a blush of pink cheek and a shadow of moustache. His eyes were dark but they shot out quick, happy lights. Among all his friends, he was the cheerful one, the outgoing one, the one who talked most to non-Hispanics. She wondered how he did in school, realizing she had no idea. She wondered if he spoke Spanish at home. She wondered where exactly he was from, and how long ago he had come to the States, and then, remembering how she could think of nothing to say to him at the dance, she scolded herself for being an idiot.

But would she skip school?

For two weeks the answer was no. Real cold set in for the first time, so that Cassie almost ran down to Wakefield Gardens to wait for Helen. Even when she wore heavy socks inside her Reeboks, her toes tingled. Who wanted to skip school and freeze to death? Still, Cassie began to carry her own money to school every day, not because she planned anything, but just for the knowledge that she could do whatever she wanted.

Toward the end of February it began to thaw. Cassie was doing well with trig, and was planning the phrasing of her request to visit Helen after school again, when Helen repeated the idea of an expedition. She was sure they wouldn't get caught. "Kids are out all the time. Half the school has the flu, anyway. Just say you had the flu and your mother is too sick to write a note."

Cassie said she would think it over.

Helen was brimming with cheerfulness as they met the next morning. "So," she said, "you brought your book bag. Maybe you can stow it in school before we go."

Had they agreed, then? "I don't think we should go into school, *if* we're going."

"Good idea. Somebody might nab us. We'll just catch the bus across the street by the mall. I know where it stops."

"So do I."

"Good. Then we're agreed." Helen beamed a smile at Cassie, whose heart skipped a beat, but okay, it was agreed.

No one bothered them as they slipped away from the crowd that was entering the school, or as they stood alone at the bus stop, or as they entered the Metrobus and dropped their coins into the fare machine. The bus door closed behind them with a soft sucking sound that made Cassie's stomach hurt; there was no backing out now.

But it was hard to stay worried. Helen described how her mother had gotten paid three times now and they had gone out to dinner, and how she was thinking of becoming a vegetarian, and how she hated fast food, and there was this great new store that sold cosmetics and soaps and stuff and didn't do *any* animal testing.

"My dad used to go hunting when he was a kid," Cassie admitted. "I bet he would still do it, if he got a chance. Isn't that disgusting? I would never do that. Would you ever shoot anything?"

"Never. Hey, remember that old Beatles song, she's leaving home, bye-bye." Helen giggled, waving at nobody out the window.

"My mom has about ten old Beatles tapes, she listens to that all the time." Cassie began to sing softly. "She's leaving home after living at home for so many years."

"What if we were leaving home, really?"

"*Your* mother would be in big trouble."

Helen laughed gaily. "She'd probably sleep too late to get to work."

"Sleep too late, meet your fate."

"Don't be late, make them wait."

"Hey, we could do rap."

"I hate rap, don't need a map."

"Look, there's the Pentagon. My dad is there right now."

"Wouldn't he be surprised if we dropped in."

Cassie rolled her eyes in answer. She wasn't as good at it as Helen. Helen had big, wide eyes that showed lots of white when she rolled them, but Cassie felt as if her eyes were too narrow.

They got off at K Street. Helen suddenly jumped up, grabbed Cassie's arm, and said, "This is it." It didn't seem right to Cassie; she thought you would be able to see the Smithsonian buildings all around them, but here she didn't recognize anything. But Helen said the bus wouldn't go directly onto the Mall anyway.

K Street was busy, with office buildings and fancy

shops at street level, and people with briefcases hurrying toward their workplaces. The sight of them reminded Cassie that she was not hurrying to English class, and she was glad when Helen pulled her arm purposefully. Helen stopped a woman almost immediately and asked her which way the Mall was. The woman pointed up a side street. "About half a mile that way," she said.

So they set off, Cassie's useless book bag weighing down her shoulder, Helen talking about how she would like to try skydiving someday, when a young man with an enormous dirty tie and filthy pants sagging around his hips blocked their way on the sidewalk. He held out a rough hand, palm up, swaying a little. "Help me," he said, looking Cassie straight in the eye. Cassie tried to notice what Helen was going to do. Helen turned her body at an angle and slipped by, leaving Cassie still confronted with the guy, who didn't move his feet. She wanted to give him something, but then she would have to unfasten all the straps on her bag and dig out her wallet and extract some coins from it, and he would be there watching her do all that. What if he grabbed the whole wallet? She stepped sideways, a wide step, shrinking from the possibility that he would sway into her, but she got around, and Helen was waiting for her. The man swore, not too loudly.

"Don't you hate that?" said Helen.

"Totally. Poor guy. He's probably homeless."

They arrived at last at Constitution Avenue, where the geography was familiar to Cassie. They headed straight for the art gallery.

"You want to look at modern stuff or old stuff?" Cassie asked, gaining confidence. She knew that the museum was divided, and that the modern glass building with the sharp angles was called the East Wing.

"Modern, most definitely."

The granite steps to the East Wing were almost empty, and this turned out to be because the museum opened at ten. It was ten minutes after nine. "I knew this," said Cassie. "I forgot."

"So what? We can just sit here. See the fountain?"

They crossed the open area, with its cobblestones laid out in fan shapes, and went over to the jets of water that shot up over their heads, spilled onto the cobblestones, ran down tiny granite steps, and seemed to disappear. "This is majorly architectural," said Helen.

"I knew you would like it."

They sat near the fountain for a long time, watching pigeons, cabs, a messenger on a bicycle, another homeless man who was asleep under a filthy blanket near a heating grate, and bits of litter that blew here and there in the breeze. It was chilly, but not really cold.

"Wish you were in school?" Cassie asked.

"No way."

Finally the museum did open, and the girls pushed through the heavy glass revolving doors. Inside, the space was so large that the tree growing in the lobby seemed small. High above, under the skylights, the red-and-black plates of a mobile moved very slightly, or perhaps that was just the dizziness you got from looking up at them. Voices from all over blurred into a punctuated hum, with an occasional sharp clatter of dishes from a restaurant at the top. Cassie was distracted by people. She watched a sleeping baby, two fat people holding hands, and a white-haired woman in a red wool jacket with a Smithsonian shopping bag.

Cassie and Helen agreed that what they liked best of all was an oversize sculpture of four girls dancing. The dancers were completely white and faceless, and seemed to be made out of papier-mâché, but their bodies looked happy, arms out and one of them balancing on one leg. When they got back outside, they tried to pose like one of the dancers, but they couldn't hold still the way papier-mâché did and they wobbled over the curbstones, laughing.

"I always wanted dance lessons, didn't you?" asked Helen.

"I'm so clumsy, I could never take dance lessons."

Cassie sat down in a bit of sunshine on the corner of a marble step, flopped her book bag off her tired shoulder, and took her shoes off. The sun was warm now. "Let's draw on our shoes," she said. "I have markers in my book bag." Almost seriously, she began coloring one toe purple, and then made green stripes across the arch. Helen stood and watched.

"Aren't you a little old for coloring?"

"Hey, if that sculptor wasn't too old for papier-mâché, I can do anything."

"I'm going over there to that stand to buy Cokes." Helen returned with a straw in her nose, moaning slightly. "Oh Lord, my time is near, release me from this hospital bed."

"Your time isn't near, you have to drink your Coke first. See my shoe? Isn't it artistic?"

"Are you going to do the other one?"

"I don't think so." Cassie put her shoes back on, noticing suddenly that two young Japanese men she'd seen in the museum were standing near them, taking pictures. "You better take that straw out of your nose."

"Do you think I will get microbiotic organisms in my soda now?"

"I think you will get into a Japanese picture of what American girls act like."

The young men were, in fact, looking at the girls, exchanging glances with each other, conferring in Japanese. Then one of them stepped over and asked, in very good English, whether this was the National Gallery of Art.

Cassie answered that it was.

"We saw you in the museum. You are art students?" The second man came over now, apparently emboldened by the first.

Cassie looked at Helen for help, and Helen said, without skipping a beat, "Yeah, we take classes at the Corcoran, we're studying Matisse right now. Did you see the Matisse?"

"Oh yes, oh yes, very beautiful."

The second man nodded his agreement, beaming. Cassie tried to hide her shoe behind her leg.

"And what is in this museum?" the man asked.

Cassie answered this time. "That's the West Wing, it's the old part of the gallery. It has art from everywhere, the Renaissance, medieval times, everything."

"Ah, I see. We want to see American artists. Can we find some here?"

"I guess so. Yes." Cassie shrugged, unable to remember who any American artists were.

"We'll help you find them," suggested Helen.

Both of the young men bubbled over with appreciation, and that was how it happened that Cassie and Helen ended up looking at yet more art, rather more than they wanted, in the company of two very interesting young men, who said that they were from the city of Osaka, in Japan, where they worked in horticultural engineering. They seemed delighted by everything, and then asked the girls to lunch in the cafeteria, and insisted on paying for it.

Helen nudged Cassie with delight, in the cafeteria line. "Jeez, how old do you think they are?"

"At least twenty."

"This is formidable."

And yet something in Cassie wished that the men hadn't paid for lunch.

They sat near a wall of falling water, which was the underside of the outdoor fountain. Helen was the one who thought of things to talk about. "I really shouldn't be eating this hamburger. I never eat beef anymore. Did you read about what they do to beef? They put hormones in the cows' feed, it's like these female hormones, and it makes you mature before you're supposed to."

"Americans eat too much animal fat, have heart trouble," said one of them, touching his chest.

"Japan, too, nowadays," said the other. "We have McDonald's."

"Estrogen," said Helen, "that's the name of the hormone. And it's in milk, too, you shouldn't drink too much milk, even if you're pregnant."

Cassie wished Helen would not talk about female bodies. One of the men put his hamburger down on his plate and looked at the waterfall, but the other one seemed very interested.

"And you refuse to eat these products?" he asked. "You are so well informed. We hear Americans are not informed, but I think perhaps this is not so."

"Yeah, we're not like Japan, in Japan everybody just works for these big companies and is completely conformist, right?" said Helen.

"What time is it?" asked Cassie. "We have to be back, don't forget." She looked at her own watch and jumped. It was after two. How long would it take to get home?

"Oh yeah." Helen looked at hers and seemed to have the same thought. "Wow, we better split."

"You are late?" asked the talkative one. "No

problem. We have a car. We can drive you some-place. Where do you have to go?"

"It's all right," said Cassie. "Thanks, we'll be all right." She remembered her book bag from under the table.

"No, we drive you. You return to school now?"

"No, we have to go home, it's way out in Arlington, you don't want to drive all the way out there."

"It's no problem, no problem." He seemed determined; he even took Helen by the arm, lead-ing her toward the exit. Cassie followed with the second man behind her. They seemed perfectly nice, but she felt uneasy.

"I think I'd rather take Metro," Cassie announced firmly, stopping as they got outside.

"Hey, come on, Cass," Helen wheedled. "Look, it's almost two-thirty. By the time you walk way down there to the Metro stop, and wait for a train, and then you have to walk about a mile home at the other end, no, more, you'll be so late."

Cassie hesitated. She was afraid this was true. She looked at the smiling men, with their neat good looks and clean suits. They wouldn't do anything wrong.

"Hey, don't make me go alone," added Helen more softly.

Cassie couldn't do that, and the man kept up a running encouragement about how close his car was, as they walked along. It wasn't all that close, Cassie thought, as they left the Mall. The man was explaining how you couldn't park at all in Japanese cities. They did at last reach a clean white compact car, a Toyota, Cassie noticed with a smile.

The talkative one drove. He had some consultations with the other in Japanese, in the front seat, which included some hand waving and pointing, and Helen said, "It's in Arlington, just across the river," which caused them both to nod in agreement.

They waited a long time at traffic lights in the city, but finally they did cross the river and got onto suburban highways, and Helen did not talk anymore about bodies. They drove past the airport, and just a little beyond, the driver announced that they were in Arlington.

"No," said the other one, "Alexandria."

"Yes, Alexandria. Your home is in Alexandria." Waiting at another light, he turned hopefully to the girls.

Cassie sat upright in alarm. "No, it isn't. It's in Arlington."

"It's across the river?" he asked incredulously.

Helen was looking hopefully at Cassie, as if she should know.

"I think they're both across the river," Cassie said anxiously. "But we live in Arlington, you have to take us to Arlington."

"Oh, Arlington." The light turned green and the car went forward, everyone silent. The quiet one turned to Cassie. "Which way is it?"

"I don't know."

"Maybe we should call your parents," he suggested, as much to his friend as to Cassie. She looked at Helen, who was shaking her head vigorously.

"I think it's up that way," said Helen, pointing at a road, obviously at random.

"Oh look," said the driver happily. "Here is our

motel." He pulled into a Quality Inn right there on the highway, took an empty parking space, and grinned at them. "So, no problem. You can come in and pretty soon we call your parents."

Cassie gripped Helen's arm, and saw that even Helen was hesitating now. But what could they do? Cassie wondered wildly what it would cost to take a cab, but she had no experience of cabs and no idea how far away they were.

The driver got out, wasting no time, and opened the back door for Helen, who sat still.

And then Cassie had a brainstorm. She remembered that when her father went on trips, he sometimes got back from the airport on Metro. "You could just take us back to the airport," she said. "We just passed it. We'll catch Metro from there."

"Don't you have a map?" asked Helen. She showed her watch to Cassie; it was 3:10. School was almost out, and Cassie was supposed to come directly home.

The driver smiled. "Sure, we have a map, up in the room. Come on upstairs." He pulled the key out of his pocket and waved it at her, smiling.

"You don't need to do that!" said Cassie, hearing the fear in her own voice but unable to stop. "You can just take us to the airport, see, it's right there. It's just a few blocks up there. Please! Take us to the airport."

"Don't be afraid!" the man wheedled at her.

That was the last straw. Cassie jumped out her side of the car, pulling Helen after her, nearly pulling Helen onto her knees on the asphalt. "Come on, we're walking to the airport. Good-bye. Thank you. Good-bye." She walked as fast as she could, not letting go of Helen, and only glancing over her shoulder once, to see the noisy one start to follow, and the quiet one stop him. They were on a public street; they could always call for help now.

But they didn't have to. No one followed them. It was a long walk to the airport, much longer than it had looked from the motel, and then after it was easy to find the Metro station, it was a long wait for a train. Cassie had left her book bag in the car, with her wallet and math book and Latin book (how was she going to explain that?), but fortunately Helen had enough change to buy a couple of Metro fares.

It was after five when Cassie walked in her front door.

"I went shopping after school with Susan, and I lost track of the time," she said immediately, just as planned, before her mother could even ask.

"Forget it," answered her mother from behind a newspaper. "The school called to ask why you were out. Helen was out, too."

9

Cassie went straight to her room and did not come down for dinner, although her mother called for her. She didn't want to see her father at all, and she didn't want to have one of those meals where they all pretended to be interested in something else. She thought about Helen, at her apartment; Meredith was probably cackling away as Helen told their adventures. Why couldn't Cassie's house be like that? She couldn't even do homework because she didn't have her books.

Around eight o'clock her mother came up with some dinner on a plate. Cassie did want to eat it, but she was disappointed when her mother sat down beside her on the bed. "You have to watch me eat?" Cassie mumbled.

"No, but I want to talk."

"Go ahead." Cassie stuffed a bite of potato into her mouth.

"I want to hear what you did."

Cassie rolled her eyes, taking her time with the food. Finally she answered, "No, you don't. You just want to prove how stupid and bad Helen is, and what a *bad* influence."

"Try me."

"We went up to New York Avenue and bought crack cocaine from a nice-looking young man on the corner. You realize, of course, that we're much too smart ever to get involved with speed."

Her mother began to laugh. "I actually thought you were too smart to smoke cigarettes. And so you are. What did you do, really?"

This was beginning to be fun. "We took skydiving lessons. Then we dropped into the White House grounds and got arrested. That's why we were late. They're going to call you later."

"Oh, they called already. I told them not to worry, your father works at the Pentagon and he's hoping you'll grow up to be a spy. Then what did you do?"

"We bought a can of spray paint and wrote our names all over the ladies' room of the Supreme Court."

"But you washed your hands when you were finished, right?"

Cassie began to laugh. "All right, so we went to the National Gallery of Art. We sat around waiting for it to open, then we looked at pictures, especially this great statue of girls dancing. Did you ever see it? Then we got some lunch."

Cassie stopped smiling, thinking about what happened next. She backtracked instead. "On the way in, we got off at the wrong bus stop, and we had to walk a long ways. And this homeless guy stopped me. It makes me feel bad, you know?"

Her mother nodded. "Me, too."

"I didn't know what to do. My money was all packed away in my backpack, so I just went past, like Helen did."

"Most of them won't hurt you."

"I know. But I feel like I hurt them. Do you ever give them money?"

"Sometimes. You know, at work I try to help people who might be homeless, if they don't find work."

"Do you think Helen's mom could ever be homeless?"

"Possibly. But I doubt it. For one thing, she could always go back to Minnesota. Homeless people usually don't have family, or else they've had huge long fights with family. And Helen seems like a pretty bright, independent girl. She'll help her mom, as she gets older."

These words of praise for Helen soothed Cassie tremendously. So her mother did see Helen's good side, after all. "She helps her already. She's *real* independent. Actually, today she kind of picked up these men, they were, like, I don't know, Japanese or something. We kind of went around the museum together."

Her mother looked interested.

"So that made us late, and we were afraid we

might get home after the busses left, and they heard us talking, and they were, like, hey, we'll drive you home, and Helen says, sure, that's great."

Her mother nodded.

"So we went to this car, and they were driving, but pretty soon it turned out they didn't have any idea where Arlington is, I mean I guess I figured something was wrong when we went past the airport."

Her mother's eyebrows shot up.

"They had Arlington and Alexandria mixed up. And all of a sudden we pull into this motel—"

Her mother suddenly blew like a jack-in-the-box. Her little listening smile faded and she shrieked. "They brought you to a motel! You little fools! You got into a car with some strange men and you drove calmly off in the wrong direction! What in the world were you thinking of? Don't you have any sense *at all*? How old were these men?"

Cassie drew back on the bed, holding her plate between herself and her mother. "I told you how it happened," she began patiently.

"But you didn't tell me how it could conceivably

happen, that two bright girls could do something so stupid. So it was Helen's idea to pick these guys up, huh?"

"No, it wasn't Helen's idea to pick them up. It wasn't a pickup. Mom, they just came over and asked us something. Did you want us to be rude?"

"There are some situations in which rudeness is the correct response."

"Mom, these were two perfectly nice, polite young guys. Maybe twenty years old. Two of them, together, not one creepy drunk with his fly coming down. What do you think? They had on suits and ties."

"Well, that is a guarantee, isn't it?" Her mother crossed her arms and stood up. "Look, let me put it this way. Did you feel, during this adventure, that everything was going according to your own plan?"

Angrily, Cassie took another bite and didn't answer.

"Did you feel really good as you got into that car? Or did you feel that you were doing something because Helen was there, that you wouldn't have done on you own?"

"Look, just shut up, okay?"

Surprisingly, her mother did shut up then. She paced up and down the room a couple of times, and then looked out the window. She spoke to the trees. "You're fourteen now, Cassie, and I can't protect you all the time, the way I did. I have to rely on your good sense. You've been all over the world, and you know how things are. You've seen that bad things can happen to people. Helen may be brave, or amusing, or whatever it is you see in her, but that doesn't mean she's the best friend for *you*. And I want you to think about that."

"Right, Mom, I'll think," Cassie answered sarcastically.

"All right then." Her mother heaved a great sigh. "Dad is ready to do math with you."

"I don't have my book."

"Why not?"

"Because I left it in . . ." Cassie had almost told the truth, but thought better of it. She wasn't about to describe the scene where she pulled Helen out of the car. "I left all my books at school."

"All right then. Bring it all home tomorrow."

Cassie waited for the wave of relief that was supposed to come when her mother left the room, but nothing happened. The food hurt her stomach, and she set the half-finished plate under her bed. She didn't want to think, she wanted to go to sleep, but she didn't want to put her head down. She turned on her tape player but she didn't hear the music. She saw, again, the homeless man, swaying, threatening to sway against her. She saw the hand held out. She saw the clean, elegant hand holding the car door for her, inviting her in. She saw her own hand, pulling frantically at Helen, getting her out of there. Her heart beat fast again, just remembering.

What would have happened? Maybe they were really nice people; maybe they had tried to help, but been lost. Maybe they would have gone upstairs and called her parents. Maybe they would have pulled out a knife and raped them. No, that was too bizarre; her mother was crazy.

Cassie felt betrayed by her mother, who had pretended to be in a good mood, had played friendly, just in order to get her to confess, so she could attack afterward. Her mother thought she was a little idiot.

Cassie started to cry. Maybe she was a little idiot. She would never confess anything again. She would never have a friend again. She would never trust Helen again. It was true, Helen had gotten them in trouble. If she had never met Helen, none of this would ever have happened.

Here she was hating Helen, and it was all her mother's fault. It was everybody's fault. It was those stupid men. I hate everybody, Cassie said to herself. I hate my mother, I hate my father, I hate the kids at school, I hate Ricardo, I hate Mr. McCutcheon, I hate Mr. Raffensberger, I hate Helen. No, I don't. Yes. I don't know. I don't know anything, and I'm such a little idiot.

She did not call Helen; she put her pajamas on, threw her stuffed animals onto the floor, and went to sleep.

Helen was not in school the next day. Sharon and Grace were sticking decals onto their nails in the girls' room, howling with laughter, and Mr.

McCutcheon was the most boring he had ever been in his life. Paragraphs. Every paragraph has a topic sentence. Blah blah blah.

Cassie quickly skimmed through part of their new novel, *Great Expectations,* and found a paragraph without a topic sentence. She raised her hand. "Mr. McCutcheon, I found this paragraph, would you look at it? I can't seem to find the topic sentence." Mr. McCutcheon read it aloud, harrumphed several times, read it again to himself, and announced that literature often works in different ways. He went back to sketching paragraph structure on the board.

Cassie skimmed through the grammar book until she found a paragraph without a topic sentence, which she called to everyone's attention.

He looked very annoyed this time. "Once in a while you just have to take my word for something," he growled.

"Why?" asked Cassie, trying to put on a sweet and innocent air.

Lucky for him, the bell rang.

In biology, things only got worse. Ricardo completely ignored her. Mr. Raffensberger was trying to explain sexual reproduction in plants, mumbling every time he had to say "sexual." He asked a question, which, as usual, no one volunteered to answer, and then he called on Cassie. "What is the scientific name for flowering plants?"

Cassie hadn't opened her biology book for days, and she had no idea. Then Ricardo raised his hand. "It's the angiosperms, Mr. Raffensberger."

The biology teacher nodded and smiled at him, and suddenly Cassie felt angrier than ever. "What was that word?" she asked, without raising her hand.

"Angiosperm, the angiosperms, it's right here in the book," he said, tapping the page the way he did for hopeless students.

Then Cassie lost it. "Sperm, did you say sperm, Mr. Raffensberger? Are you sure you want to say that word?"

Mr. Raffensberger turned red, while one of the leather jacket boys let out a whistle. Cassie felt impelled onward. "I didn't know they had sperm all over the flowers. Yuck! All those sperm trying to get to the eggs, just like in people."

"People have to be married," he snapped, but he had misjudged his class, which burst out laughing.

"Oh, married," said Cassie sarcastically. "I guess I *forgot.*" She smacked her book closed, looking around. Mr. Raffensberger was hesitating over his big poster of flower parts, so Cassie took over.

"What's that thing there, that gametophyte?" she called out. "That female gametophyte? Is that like a transvestite, or what?"

The guys began laughing and hooting, looking back at Cassie with admiration, and up at Mr. Raffensberger to see what he would do. He seemed transfixed by this transformation in his best student; his hand trembled slightly as he picked the poster up to remove it, then changed his mind and set it back on the tray below the blackboard. He opened his mouth, but before he could speak, Cassie called out again. "Does this happen in all the flowers, Mr. Raffensberger? How come they call it the birds and the bees, wouldn't it be better to call it the birds and the flowers? God, think about it, I'm never picking daisies again."

Mr. Raffensberger turned crimson under his

wrinkled skin, but Cassie could not stop. A weight was lifting off her; all the forbidden words, all the forbidden subjects, all the forbidden behavior was rolling out of her, and she was somewhere else, watching, and glad. She had been good long enough. Let them deal with her, let them figure out what to do. She was surprised when the bell rang, and she went right on sitting there, half expecting the class to applaud.

But they didn't, they dashed out of their seats the way they always did, and only Cassie was left behind, turned to stone. School was over, and even Mr. Raffensberger left quickly, not looking at her.

Someone touched Cassie, and she looked up to see Ricardo. She grinned, but he did not grin back, only looked at her earnestly. "You're going to get in trouble," he said, almost roughly.

"I don't care." She tried to grin again.

"You don't care?" He sat in the seat next to her, putting his face within inches of hers. She felt his breath, smelling very lightly of milk. "You don't care if you get in trouble? That's being like Manny. What's the matter with you? All this time you study, you pay attention, and suddenly you have an attitude."

"I'm having a bad time," Cassie explained weakly. "See, Helen got me in trouble. We skipped school and went downtown, and there were these two guys that offered to drive us home. My parents think Helen is this bad influence on me."

"And she is, right?"

"Oh, no!" Cassie stood up, ready to leave. "Helen is my best friend. She's my only real friend."

"She's your only friend?" Ricardo looked at her as if she had said something in a foreign language. "You're not friends with Susan? Grace? Rebecca? All these girls . . ." He shook his head.

Cassie stepped away from him. "I couldn't be friends with Susan."

"Why not? She's a good student, like you. At least you used to be a good student."

"I'm not like Susan!" Cassie started to leave, but Ricardo's voice held her at the door.

"Well, you better quit being rude to Mr. Raffensberger."

"Yeah. Thanks. I'll act better. I guess I better go now."

"See ya round, Cassie."

"Bye." She walked uncertainly back to her locker, grateful that it was the last period, and now she could go home.

10

That evening the telephone kept ringing. There were two calls for Cassie's father, one for her mother, and then it was Helen, sounding scared, saying that her mother had lost her job and maybe they were going back to Minnesota. Cassie started to cry.

"Oh God, not you, too." Helen was trying to be flippant, but she sounded tired.

"Me too what?"

"Crying. That's all my contemptible mother does, every time I ask her what happened."

"Your mother isn't contemptible. How would you

like to come home and you get nothing but blame just because these two jerks can't tell Arlington from Alexandria?"

"What?"

Cassie tried to fill Helen in on how her mother had reacted to their little trip, but Helen didn't seem to be really listening. She said, "Yeah, right" from time to time, without any conviction, until Cassie stopped talking altogether, and they were both silent on the line.

Finally Helen said, "If she'd just stop crying, she could get another job."

Cassie tried to picture Meredith in the apartment, but it was hard, and she wanted to get on to telling Helen about Ricardo. "Doesn't she stop crying at all?"

"Oh yeah, she does. But she's just, you know, kind of exasperating."

"Maybe she'll be better in a couple of days," Cassie tried.

"Maybe. Well, talk to ya later."

Cassie felt bad. She knew she had not comforted Helen, but she didn't know what else to say. Maybe

Meredith would be better off back home with relatives. Then Helen would have other people to depend on, too.

But what would happen to Cassie, if Helen left?

The phone rang again and Cassie picked it up, hoping it was Helen again with something better to say. But a male voice said that he was Dr. Gosling and he would like to speak to Mr. or Mrs. Winn. Dr. Gosling was the principal.

Cassie's mother took the phone. She didn't say much, except "I see." After a little she put her hand over the speaker to say that Cassie was suspended until they came in for a conference. Her father said calmly that in that case, they would be there at 8:30 in the morning. Late at night, Cassie heard her parents' voices, tense, disagreeing, up and down, then soft.

The conference was blessedly brief. Both her parents came, shook hands with Dr. Gosling, and sat in the very seats where they had sat when Cassie was enrolled in the school and praised for her impressive record. Cassie pushed her chair as far back from Dr. Gosling's desk as possible without making a big show of it. Dr. Gosling began, looking very relaxed. He said that Cassie was a fine student who seemed to be having a rough period, which was not at all out of the ordinary for young people of this age. All the adults nodded wisely.

"Is there anything you would like to explain to us?" Dr. Gosling asked Cassie.

Cassie said no.

"Do you *know* why you were so rude to Mr. . . . Mr. . . . your biology teacher?" urged her mother.

Cassie flashed up again. "He's not a very good teacher." She looked straight at Dr. Gosling as she said it.

The principal met her look calmly, but his hands did a washing movement on his desktop. "Mr. Raffensberger has been with the school system for nearly thirty years," he said.

Cassie made a movement of disgust, but he went on seriously.

"When he began his career, this school was not even in existence. The entire system was composed of three elementary schools and one secondary. The student body was more uniform and classes were much smaller. Mr. Raffensberger has adapted to more change than I ever hope to see in my lifetime, and I have a whole file full of letters from students who were grateful to him. His wife died of cancer about ten years ago, and one of his sons was killed in Vietnam. This is his last year as a teacher, and I would hope that he could leave with a feeling of reward. Sometimes the old are not exactly to the taste of the young"—he smiled condescendingly at Cassie—"but Mr. Raffensberger has been an outstanding teacher, and I will not allow his classes to be disrupted during his last months as a teacher."

Cassie looked at the floor. She thought about telling him the class was disrupted half the time anyway, but decided against it. "All right," she said.

"And," he finished cheerfully, "I would like Cassie to write a letter of apology. And with the understanding that that will be on my desk by tomorrow, I don't see any reason why Cassie can't join her classes immediately."

Her parents nodded and smiled and stood up and shook hands again.

"To Mr. Raffensberger?" Cassie asked.

"Yes, to Mr. Raffensberger." He showed them to the door, and her father kissed her good-bye in the hall.

Cassie dragged her way into English, which was almost over. Sharon nearly accosted her as soon as the bell rang. "I heard what you did in biology. Wow, that was formidable. Did you have to go to Dr. Gosling? What'd he say?"

Cassie wanted to get away, but something held her. "He said I have to write a letter of apology to Hamburger."

Sharon laughed again. "That's all? Wow, you got off easy. That's because you're such a good student. If I did that, he'd suspend me for a week. So, have you written it yet?"

"No, I just got out of there."

They scattered to their classes, and Cassie spent math, where she had no book, trying to compose a letter. "Dear Mr. Raffensberger, even though you are such a crummy teacher I don't mind because at least you're going to retire. Dear Mr. Raffensberger, I'm sorry about your wife and your son but it's not my fault. Dear Mr. Raffensberger, now you know the difference between Susan Carpenter and me."

She turned over her notebook paper and tried to do it sincerely, but the words wouldn't come. It was worse when she got to biology and actually looked at the man. He was ugly. He didn't know what he was talking about. He didn't dare call on her, and kept shooting worried glances in her direction. He couldn't control the noisy kids. And Ricardo was not looking at her at all. Not even Susan spoke to her, but instead looked at her almost with awe.

At the end of school Cassie went to her locker alone. She stared at her small stack of books, wondering if the library would have the math book so she could at least do her homework. Eventually she would have to pay for it, and for the Latin book. She would take biology home, the heavy old thing. She slung it into the old backpack she was using now, and walked alone through the crowded halls, and alone down the steps, looking at her feet.

"Hey, Cassie!"

She looked up.

"Hey, Cassie!" It was Sharon, running. "Hey, Gracie and I are going across the road to Roy's, wanna come?"

Cassie stared for a moment, uncertainly.

"Yeah, okay." Cassie shifted her backpack and followed Sharon down the steps, beside Grace.

At Roy's they ordered a box of chicken nuggets together and argued over the sauce, and took it to a table beside some other kids from school, Sara and Rebecca and Steve and Peter Hofnagle. After a lot of chatter, Rebecca suddenly said, "Hey, Cassie, I heard about you and Mr. Raffensberger."

They all got quiet and looked at her. Cassie flinched inwardly for a moment, but there was no way out but to say something.

"I guess I got kind of carried away."

They laughed as if she had said something very witty, and then Sara said, "Did you hear what she *said*? Mr. Raffensberger says you have to be *married* to have sex, and Cassie's like, oh, I *forgot*." They all laughed harder.

"What did Gosling say?" asked Grace, more quietly.

"She has to write him a letter of apology," Sharon answered for her. "I wish I could get off that easy sometimes."

Cassie smiled at them all shyly. "It's hard," she admitted.

She saw Steve and Grace and several others

nodding. "It doesn't have to be long," Steve suggested.

"Let's write it for her," said Sharon, pulling out a piece of paper. "Here, Cassie, you write."

Cassie took a pen that someone handed her and held it over the paper, looking around expectantly.

"Dear Big Mac," Sharon began.

"Why don't you just give him an invitation to Family Life Education?" Sara asked. "He could use a little."

"Dr. Gosling said his wife died of cancer," Cassie suddenly remembered.

The group fell silent a moment, like a horse reined in.

"Well, that kind of spoiled everything," said Rebecca. "I gotta go, guys, catch you later."

The group began to break up, and Cassie's paper was still empty. But Sharon and Grace stayed. "You really have to write it today?" Grace asked.

Gripping her pen, Cassie nodded. "Dear Mr. Raffensberger," she wrote firmly. "I am sorry that I was rude in your class. I won't do it again. Sincerely, Cassandra Winn." She laid the pen down. It was simple.

"You have to take it to him?" Sharon asked.

"I have to give it to Dr. Gosling. I might as well go do it now, before I go home."

"All right. See you tomorrow."

On their way out the door they nearly bumped into two guys who seemed to know Sharon. "Hey, you leaving already?" asked one, playfully pulling at her backpack. "Who's this?" He looked at Cassie, not unfriendly.

"It's Cassie, you know, Helen's best friend."

"Oh yeah, her." The boys went on into the restaurant, and in a moment Cassie and Sharon had turned different ways.

Cassie's feelings tumbled inside her, making no sense. She was famous for making cutting remarks to Mr. Raffensberger, which wasn't all good, but it wasn't all bad, either. At least she was famous. And Sharon and Grace liked her, and maybe other kids, too. And now the letter was written and that was all over, and she didn't have to think about it anymore. But something else was bugging her. It was the way Sharon had introduced her. Why, what was wrong with it? Only that Sharon had introduced her as Helen's best friend, as if that were all she was.

Cassie entered the school office very quietly, handed her letter (folded) to a secretary, and started for home. She guessed she would take Jamie for a walk.

But her mother was already home when she got there, and Jamie and a friend were bombarding a plastic castle with little rubber cannonballs. Cassie went upstairs to call Susan to get the math problems from her. Susan read all fifteen of them over the phone, patiently, and then she, too, asked about Cassie's punishment. Susan seemed to think that writing a letter of apology was pretty hard.

"It was hard," Cassie admitted. "First it was hard because I wasn't sorry, and then it was hard because I was."

"You mean you are sorry?"

"Yeah, I am." It was a great relief to say this. Cassie repeated all she knew about Mr. Raffensberger's life.

"But that's not your fault," Susan argued reasonably. "I mean, you were always right, he is a bad teacher, and you kind of lose patience."

"*You* never do."

"Well, maybe I should. I understood when you did that, anyway."

"Did you?"

"Well, yeah."

Helen was back in school the next day, but not really herself. She was quiet and she paid attention in English, and Cassie did not really talk to her until lunchtime, and then only because they ran into each other in the bathroom. Helen was mad.

"So, I guess you found some other kids to eat lunch with."

"They just came and sat with me. What am I supposed to do?"

"Quite the popularity kid." Helen was looking in the mirror, applying purple lip gloss to her lips.

"No, I'm not. You can come and sit with us if you want."

"Oh, *thank* you so much."

Cassie bought an apple and went back to the table where Sharon, Rebecca, and Grace were sitting, and to her surprise Helen followed her, with an ice-cream sandwich. Helen sat down defiantly. Sharon and Grace stopped their chatter and stared at her, and for a moment Cassie was afraid they were going to be rude. But Grace only said, "Wow, you're lucky you can eat ice cream, you're so thin."

"I suppose I should eat *healthy* food, like your friend Cassie," said Helen spitefully.

Grace glanced at Sharon, and then at Cassie. It was a terrible moment; it was as if Cassie had to choose. She looked at Helen, hunched on the cafeteria bench, staring at her ice cream, drawn into herself. She looked at Grace, who looked back expectantly, curiously.

"Helen's in a bad mood," Cassie apologized.

"Who isn't?" said Grace quickly. "Don't you wish spring break was here right now?" And then the bell rang to break them up and scatter them.

The hallway was a mass of bodies going different directions, as usual. Cassie suddenly thought of the diagram of the eye, and how everything you see is upside down from the way it is, how merely by looking you can make the world tumble helter-skelter out of its place.

On the way home, after school, she saw Helen ahead of her and ran to catch up. "Are you going back to Minnesota, or what?"

"Much you care."

That was hard. "All right, so be that way."

They were silent for a while, and then Helen said, "No, we're staying. My uncle sent us some money. My mom has a therapist, and she's supposed to get a new job next week."

"Oh. That sounds good."

"It's okay."

After a pause, Helen went on. "Remember the poem? Are you nobody, too? Let's be nobodies until the end of school."

"I don't want to be a nobody," said Cassie softly. "Emily Dickinson is kind of strange, when you think about it. Remember that one you gave me? The soul selects, I forget how it goes, just one person. I don't know. I don't see why you should have just one person. Maybe the person you marry, but even so, people love their children and their parents, and their friends. . . ."

Helen was so quiet that Cassie knew Helen knew what she was saying. Finally Helen answered, "Yeah, old Emily, just shut herself up in her room. Kind of like my mother, in a way."

"Your mother sounds like she's doing better."

"Yeah, I guess so."

"I guess your mother is even more trouble than mine," Cassie said, trying to sound light.

"Your mother's good," said Helen seriously. "She makes money and she cooks meals. My mother can't even . . ." She trailed off, as if finishing that sentence was too difficult.

"I know," said Cassie, "and you do a great job of helping her. My mother is just, well, sometimes when she means to help me, she doesn't."

Helen's happy look came back for a moment. "Like when she buys you clothes." She giggled.

Cassie made a face and laughed. "That's why I need friends."

"Am I still your friend?" Helen asked.

"Yes." Cassie wished she didn't sound so hesitant. "But, Helen, you're *one* of my friends, okay? I mean, Grace and Sharon and Rebecca, and other kids, they like me, too. And they'd like you, if you'd give them a chance."

Helen tossed her hair proudly. "They don't know anything," she said vaguely.

They had reached the apartment, and Helen turned to go in.